The Fae-Child of Arran

Arran

A Royal Quest of Blood and Magic

Eliza Maddox

Contents

Prologue
Rightfully Ours

"Do you not recognize me from our wedding night, my queen?"

Queen Deirdre sat up with such a start that the nursing infant fell from her breast.

That voice. It didn't so much reach her ears as slither into them. The intruder looked just like her husband, King Athos, but the voice was not his. Far from it. This voice was strange, high and hushing like the passage of wind through the reeds.

Only a moment before, the queen had been resting, letting her soft gaze fall on the head of the nursing child. Then this creature appeared from behind the curtains, wearing the king's likeness.

Whoever—or *whatever*—it was let out a cackle like frozen twigs snapping underfoot.

Shrinking from the sound and the chill that entered through the open window, the queen tried her best to cover her naked breast. The child whimpered.

"She's still hungry. You'd best feed her."

"Rest assured, I will! Only, who are you? I demand you explain yourself!"

Before the queen's astonished eyes, the imposter underwent a change in every aspect of his appearance. The familiar auburn locks became unruly hanks of straw-like hair, and the beard vanished. The skin darkened and seemed to shimmer like the scales of a fish as the creature's limbs grew long and thin.

"Nochtan of the Narra Fae, at your service."

1

The queen moaned. Her mind was a swirl of confusion. "I don't understand, I don't understand," she repeated.

"It's simple. The child is yours. But the child is also mine. Ours. The Narra."

"What do you mean, 'yours'? She is mine! All mine! For nine months I carried her ... I feed her, I sing to her, I bathe her."

"Don't be silly. The nursemaid does the bathing. But enough of this. Please, the child."

Nochtan moved toward the bed. The queen shrunk from him.

"You can't have her!"

"Is that what the king will say?"

The fae drew closer to the bed, sitting on its edge. He reached out both hands, and the queen smelled moss and cool stone wafting from his body.

"The king ... My husband ... He will have you imprisoned for slander. He will have you killed for threatening his queen."

"Will he?" Nochtan looked amused. "And how will he lock me up, then?"

Where Nochtan had been sitting, Queen Deirdre now saw a bottlefly. The fly buzzed up to land on a corner of the four-poster bed before transforming into a raven. The raven cawed and fluttered down to the ground as Nochtan again took his original form.

"You Arran have gone far enough," he said. "And you don't seem to study your history. Not even of your own people. That child is ours by rights. I didn't even need to pretend to be your husband. That was just part of the fun."

A sob escaped the queen's lips as Nochtan took the child from her.

"Don't worry, we'll take good care of her."

Through tears, in a voice wracked by grief, Queen Deirdre managed to ask, "Will I see her again?"

"Hm. We'll think it over."

"What shall I tell the king ...?"

But Nochtan only shrugged. He opened the window. Once more he took the form of the great raven and flew off, the small bundle containing the child held tight in his beak.

There was a knock at the door. The queen caught her breath.

"Yes ...?"

"It's Lady Abria. I heard a commotion. May I enter?"

Without waiting for an answer, the king's sister strode into the bedchamber. She crossed the room and closed the open window.

"What are you thinking, Deirdre? The chill—" Lady Abria stopped talking. She looked at the queen. "Where is the child?"

It took several attempts before Queen Deirdre was able to give a coherent account. Lady Abria struggled to believe her. But the child was nowhere to be found, and the queen was in a state of shock.

"What am I going to do, Abria? The king mustn't find out."

"No, he mustn't. Under no circumstances!" A malevolent smile crept across Lady Abria's face. She had an idea. A terrible idea. "If you'll listen to me, I'll tell you just what to do ..."

Chapter 1

The Inapt Pupil

O wen's heart pounded as he sprinted toward the gondola gate, the fine leather of his boots skidding on the polished cobblestones. The gondolier had already begun to swing the heavy gate closed. On spotting the flustered prince, his eyes widened and he paused, holding the gate ajar.

"Your Highness!"

"Hello, Thalor!"

With a final burst of energy, Owen leaped forward just as the cabin door began to slide shut. He slipped through the narrow gap, his breath catching in his throat. A silvery blur entered after him and a slinky feline creature with saucer-like eyes landed deftly beside him, her showy tail brushing his arm in quiet reprimand. It was Lyr, Owen's serpine.

The gondola shuddered into motion, swaying gently as it embarked on its journey around the loop.

"Sorry, Lyr," Owen panted, reaching down to stroke her sleek head. "Nearly left you behind this time."

The serpine huffed, the sound soft yet chiding, and nudged his hand with her cold nose.

As the gondola ascended, Owen pressed his face against the cool glass. Below him sprawled the Vale of Arran, a tapestry of greens and browns unfurling beneath the morning haze. The river should be there, carving its way through the deepest part of the

4

gorge—a hidden serpent cloaked by the mist. But Owen could only guess at its path, marked by the monstrous silhouettes of lumbering machines that fed off its power.

"Always harnessing, never understanding," Owen mumbled to himself. He thought about the countless hours his professors spent lecturing on the mechanics of those contraptions—the gears, the pistons, the ceaseless grind.

"Wouldn't you rather explore it than hover above?" he whispered, more to himself than to Lyr, though she tilted her head as if pondering his question.

The serpine's tail swished in silent agreement, sending a ripple of air that smelled faintly of ozone and pine through the gondola. Owen smiled at the irony. The valley was forbidden. Etched into the very landscape of his kingdom, a realm of secrets his royal blood denied him access to.

"Father says it's dangerous, Lyr. But what isn't? Even this flying box has its perils."

Lyr nuzzled his cheek. Owen sighed, his thoughts slowly cascading like the mists below—thoughts of gorges unexplored, of lessons unlearned, of a future uncertain.

"Maybe one day. One day, I'll walk your hidden paths."

The gondola swayed gently, a cradle suspended from the heavens. Around Owen, the other students were as still as stone, their eyes devouring the pages of thick engineering handbooks with an intensity that made their indifference to the world beyond the glass almost palpable. The prince felt conspicuously alone in his idleness, his lap empty where a book should have been. Which reminded him ...

"By the Great Gears ..." Owen rummaged through his satchel in a futile search for something he knew wasn't there. Lyr perked up, sensing Owen's distress. She scampered from her perch on the seat beside him and wound herself around his neck—a living scarf of fur and empathy.

"Left them on my desk! *Again*, Lyr. This is a disaster."

Lyr mewed softly, offering solace that words could not. Owen exhaled slowly, trying to ease the tension from his shoulders as the gondola docked with a jolt that rattled his bones.

"Come on, Lyr. Let's face the music."

He stepped out into the brisk air and made his way up the broad path to the ugly stone building squatting on the hill. Inside, the academy's hallways echoed with the calm, regular footsteps of those who knew their place in the world. Owen's own hurried steps beat a tattoo of discord and tardiness.

As he slipped into the classroom, silence drew itself over the room; all eyes turned to him. The professor, a hawkish man with eyes as sharp as the tools they studied, fixed his gaze on Owen.

"Prince Owen," the professor began, his voice slicing through the quiet, "I presume there's a royal reason for your untimely arrival?"

"Apologies, Professor Carthridge," Owen stammered. "Time got away from me."

"How appropriate," Carthridge sniffed. "Our assignment was to improve the simple water clock. I trust you've brought your blueprint to share with the class?"

"I ... I don't have it, sir. I accidently left my work at home."

"Then perhaps you can enlighten us with the concept verbally?"

"Verbally, yes," Owen tried to picture his desk, littered with papers and diagrams, but found only the blank slate of his mind. "It harnesses the ... the natural flow of ... water ..."

"Enough," Carthridge cut him off, eliciting snickers from the rows of students. "Your Highness, I will not have you waste our time with unpreparedness. To the library with you. Study, so that you may at least attempt to match the dedication of your peers."

Owen retreated from the classroom, head bowed, the heat of shame on his cheeks.

"Father will hear of this," Owen thought, his heart sinking. "Another failure to add to the list."

With Lyr in the lead, Owen made his way to the library. She knew where they were going, and her pace revealed her excitement. "Lyr, you lucky beast. Always living for the moment."

He entered the musty hall whose towering shelves loomed over him like silent judges. The librarian welcomed him without a sound and led him to an alcove labeled "Remedial Studies."

"Here you are, Prince Owen."

"Thank you, Miss Elgin."

The librarian smiled sympathetically, then turned and left to continue her endless cataloging of engineering patents.

Once alone, Owen glanced at the basic texts, then let his eyes drift down to a sun-faded book set on a shelf by his feet. He reached for it and pulled it from the shelf, sending dust particles into the air. Behind the book was nothing but empty space. Part of the opening to a hidden corridor beyond.

"Come on, Lyr," he whispered, pulling more books from the lower shelf before he crawled into the passageway.

The narrow space opened into a tiny room. The prince's secret refuge, which he had discovered on his third or fourth visit to the alcove of Remedial Studies. Who knew who had created it, or what purpose it had once served ...

Over time, he had filled the room with trinkets and bric-à-brac smuggled out of the castle or found on his lonely walks through the kingswood. Yet these were of little interest compared to the shelves of ancient, leather-bound magic books. His personal collection, bought in secret from booksellers in Arrantown. Owen ran his fingers over the embossed covers, feeling the power etched in their titles, even if the knowledge within continued to elude him without the guidance of a real magician.

"Let's see what wonders we can't understand today, eh?"

Owen pulled down a heavy volume, its pages filled with arcane symbols and illustrations of mythical creatures. He traced the images, lost in their intricate detail, imagining stories where he was the master of spells, not the bumbling prince who couldn't blueprint a waterwheel.

"Wouldn't it be something, Lyr?" he mused aloud. "If I could wield magic like the heroes in these tales? We might find less destructive ways of harnessing the powers of nature ... Save the forests and valleys--change the course of Arran history!"

The serpine was nestled in her favorite nook, a miniature hammock Owen had fashioned from a napkin filched from the dining hall, knit in the alternating silver and blue pattern particular to the House of Arran.

Hours slipped by in the company of enchantments and legends until sunlight no longer filtered through the single stained-glass window, signaling the afternoon's advance. Owen reluctantly closed the last spellbook.

"Back to the castle," he said with a heavy heart, coaxing Lyr up through the secret passage, through the gloomy library and into the bright bustle of the academy.

As the gondola came to rest on the other side of the gorge, Owen felt the familiar sensations of dread curdling in his stomach. The platform came into view, and there, waiting for him, was Henrick, his footman.

Henrick wore a nervous expression, though that meant nothing in itself. The footman always looked nervous. Owen wondered what he was doing there.

"I've come to ... collect you, Your Highness. They said, erm, in case you'd forgotten. It's the dinner party, to celebrate the acquisition of the ... I'm sorry, I've forgotten the name of the bank."

"It doesn't matter, Henrick. They're all the same."

"Oh! Ha ha! A good one, my lord. Very humorous. Nevertheless, we mustn't be late. Your Highness still needs to dress."

"Yes, yes. Of course." Owen stepped onto solid ground, Lyr's tail coiled tight around his wrist, her body hugging his ribs. "Lead the way."

Henrick brought the prince to a waiting carriage, its gold leaf and royal insignia drawing the eye of the other passengers. Owen hated this kind of attention; it was the reason he had petitioned to make his own way to the gondola every morning—a request King Athos had granted begrudgingly, and to which the queen had seemed curiously opposed, as if frightened by the notion of Owen's independence.

As they rode over the royal bridge, spanning the gully between the two peaks of Arrantown, Owen thought glumly about what lay ahead. The bridge joined the town proper to the castle grounds. Every time he crossed it, the prince felt as though he was being dragged from a sweet dream into cold, unforgiving daylight.

In the carriage, Henrick tried to engage Owen in conversation, however his mind was still on the events of that afternoon. Somehow, he feared his father had already learned about his failure at the academy. Owen sometimes wondered if the king knew about his secret refuge in the library and was merely waiting for the right opportunity to snatch it away from him.

They arrived at the castle. Owen stepped down onto the gravel of the courtyard. As the guards opened the doors, he took a deep breath before crossing the threshold.

No one was there to greet him. Certainly his mother was still being powdered and teased, strapped into a corset as much against her will as Owen soon would be into the stiff velvet tunic his aunt made him wear on these occasions.

As he followed the footman to his chambers, the prince wondered for the umpteenth time if things wouldn't have been different if his sister, Princess Emyr, hadn't died so shortly after birth. He liked to imagine they would have been.

Half an hour later, scrubbed, dressed and perfumed, Owen stood outside the doors to the dining hall. He took a deep breath, tried to summon a smile, and then entered the room where every aspect of his dull, disagreeable life was to be determined from now until the crown was thrust upon him.

Immediately, his aunt, Lady Abria, and King Athos turned from the table of toadying courtiers to greet him. Owen couldn't help but feel a surge of panic. Something was off ... The expressions on their faces were too eager, too prepared.

Was it a trap?

Chapter 2

A Stray Word

The grand dining hall of Arran castle was alive with the clinking goblets and rowdy conversation that echoed under the high arched ceilings. Owen sat hunched in his chair, his tunic chafing at the collar as he picked at the venison on his plate and listened to the courtiers gossip.

"Did you hear about the Ladrian child?"

"Yes. They say she has the gift of foresight."

"Gift? More like a curse. I feel sorry for the family."

"Like Emyr," murmured Queen Deirdre, her voice barely rising over the noise of the other diners. "She always has such vivid dreams."

Owen was close enough to hear her. His fork paused mid-air. "Emyr …?"

He glanced up, searching his mother's face. She was absentmindedly tracing the rim of her wine glass, her gaze distant, caught in some unseen memory.

"Dead children do not dream, Mother."

Her eyes snapped to his, a flicker of confusion crossing her features before they softened. "Of course, my dear. It was only a slip of the tongue."

Owen nodded, frowning inwardly. Emyr was dead; a tiny tomb in the Arran mausoleum was all he had ever known of his sister. He looked with concern at his mother.

"More wine, Your Majesty?" A servant hovered at Deirdre's elbow.

"Yes, thank you."

Owen pushed his food around his plate, his appetite waning. The voices around him faded into a distant murmur, as he turned his mother's strange words over in his mind.

"Your mother simply tangled her words, Owen," Lady Abria interjected, her voice a silken thread weaving through the tension. "Grief can make anyone confuse past and present."

Her eyes, cool and calculating, locked on his for a moment, daring him to challenge this simple explanation.

"Right," he muttered, swallowing the lump in his throat along with a bite of meat that tasted like ash.

Grief? Emyr died years ago. Moreover, she was an infant, and infants don't dream. Or, if they do, they certainly don't tell their mothers.

"Let us turn our attention to more pressing concerns." The king set down his knife and fork with finality as he addressed the now-quiet room. "The Zorin surveyors continue to encroach upon our territory. Their disregard for our treaty is ... troubling."

Owen swirled the grape nectar around his goblet, the dark liquid reflecting his own unease. Treaties and politics were ever the preferred battlegrounds of the House of Arran. He could care less.

"Troubling, but not unexpected," Lady Abria said smoothly. "The strength of our guilds will keep their ambitions at bay. As for our banking interests, they extend far beyond Zorin reach."

"Engineering and riches may fortify a kingdom, sister, but alliances preserve them," King Athos countered, an edge to his words.

"Which is why our influence within the Merchant Council must remain unchallenged."

"Unchallenged and profitable," the king added, nodding. "Our future depends on it. Isn't that right, Owen?"

"Of course, Father." Owen's voice sounded distant to his own ears. His thoughts crept back to Emyr, her existence now a question mark that loomed over every word spoken.

"Do not let your focus drift from matters at hand, my son." King Athos's gaze cut through Owen, sharp as the knife that had resumed slicing through the roast venison.

"I won't, Father." He forced his gaze back onto his plate. The rich, barely-touched venison smothered in gravy taunted him. What secrets lay buried beneath the foundations of Arran?

King Athos leaned forward, eyes narrow slits of pure conviction. "It's crucial that you understand, Owen. Our lineage is the bedrock on which Arran stands."

"Understood," Owen replied, though his father's words felt like chains rather than reassurances.

"Good." The king sat back, satisfied. "Tomorrow," his voice rumbled, "we will discuss your role in securing our future."

Dread settled like a stone in Owen's stomach. Tomorrow's conversation would bear consequences, perhaps graver than any border dispute with the House of Zorin.

A sharp rap at the chamber door sliced through the tension. All eyes turned as a royal guard slipped inside with whispered urgency. Lady Abria rose, her chair scraping against the marble floor.

"Will you be long, sister?" the king asked, his voice resonating with authority that demanded an answer.

"Nothing to fret over, dear brother. Merely a trifle I must attend to."

With a swish of her long gown, she departed, leaving Owen to wonder what secrets lay beyond the reach of his kinship with her.

Several times he had seen her in conversation with Sir Galvrey, the old intelligence officer, or another of the court advisors. On the last occasion, rounding a bend in the path through the kingswoods, he had come across them speaking alone, their conversation furtive and intense. When she heard his footsteps, his aunt had looked up, clothing her mouth firmly and motioning for Galvrey to do the same.

Owen felt a stirring of suspicion now, as the question crossed his mind once more: What plots did Lady Abria weave in the shadows?

"Father," he ventured, "may I be excused? I find myself ... weary."

"Of course, Owen" Queen Deirdre replied, her gaze soft upon her son, unaware of the storm brewing within him.

"Thank you, Mother." He barely glanced at the plates of stewed pears and cream being placed in front of him. It was normally his favorite.

Rising, he nodded to his father, the weight of his expectations pressing down on him. But it was not duty that called him tonight; it was the lure of the forbidden arts, the experiments he had been forced to abandon the night before waiting silently for him in his chambers.

"No, Owen. I did not give my leave. Be seated."

The boy halted mid-step, a cold shiver crawling up his spine. His hand gripped the back of his chair, knuckles whitening.

"Father?" Owen turned, masking his dread with curiosity.

"Sit."

His father's eyes bore into him. They were so like Lady Abria's. Sharp as flint, and as unyielding. Owen's throat tightened. He lowered himself onto the chair, the velvet cushion suddenly feeling like stone beneath him.

"Can't it wait until morning?" The words tumbled out, feigned fatigue lacing his plea. "I'm quite exhausted."

"No. There is another matter I wish to discuss. Morning is too long to wait for what needs to be said tonight."

Owen's heart hammered against his ribcage. The secret library at the academy, the forbidden texts—had word reached his father's ears? His mind raced, conjuring excuses, explanations, anything that might shield him from his father's wrath.

"Your studies have come to my attention," the king began.

Owen's breath hitched. Sweat gathered at his brow. He wanted to look away but knew better than to show weakness.

"Indeed, Father?"

"Indeed." Athos leaned forward, hands clasped upon the table, the candlelight casting shadows over his stern features.

Owen swooned, feeling the walls of the dining hall closing in.

"The boy does look tired. Can we not let him rest? There will be time tomorrow for us to speak with him." Queen Deirdre appeared suddenly sober. The concern in her appeal was genuine. Owen felt grateful.

King Athos glared at her. "Out," he barked, the word cutting through the air like a dagger.

The queen's gaze moved from her husband to her son, her eyes wide with a fear that Owen knew too well. She rose and departed without protest, sending her son one last look of sympathy.

The door closed with a thud. All that remained was the uncomfortable shifting of courtiers in their seats. It was what Athos wanted. To humiliate his son without the presence of the one person who might stand up for him.

"Father—"

"Silence."

Owen's hands clenched one another beneath the table. The blood reached his temples, pulse pounding in his ears, a mixture of fear and impotent rage.

"Your disobedience is a stain on our family name," Athos growled.

"Disobedience?" Owen fought to keep his voice steady.

"Secret studies. Forbidden knowledge—if you can call such gobbledygook knowledge at all!"

Once again, Owen searched for an excuse, any lifeline. But nothing came. The walls of the dining hall seemed to press closer, the ornate tapestries seemed ready to smother him.

"Your future as my heir is at risk," Athos continued, his tone laced with menace.

"Please, father. I meant no harm."

"Meant no harm?" The king stood abruptly, his chair scraping back violently. "You defy me!"

"Never intentionally." But Owen's words sounded hollow even to his own ears.

"Intention is irrelevant!"

The candles fluttered and sputtered desperately, as if trembling before the king's wrath.

"Tomorrow," Athos hissed, "you will learn the consequences of your actions."

"Consequences?"

"Grave consequences. For you and for that creature you keep. Yes, especially for her. I've been looking for an anniversary gift for your mother. A new stole would do nicely."

Owen gasped. "Mother would never—"

"Enough! Leave us."

The prince stood, his legs trembling. He stepped back, one cautious step at a time, until he reached the door.

"Remember," his father called out behind him, "the blood of Arran flows through you, but it can be tainted by one's own deeds."

The servant opened the door. Owen stumbled into the corridor, the sounds of the dinner party resuming behind him. He fled down the hallway.

As the distance between him and his father grew, so did the knot of dread in his stomach. What punishment awaited him at sunrise? Would his pursuit of forbidden knowledge cost him his birthright, or worse, Lyr's life?

Chapter 3

Orphaned

S houting. Commotion.

Owen's eyes flew open and were met with the darkness of his unlit chamber. It was still night. He didn't recall falling asleep. Yet there he was, one arm flung across his desk, wiping a slick of drool from his mouth as his heart thumped against his ribs. Lyr stirred from her curled position at the foot of the bed, ears erect, alert.

The sounds came again. Guards calling out. Confusion in the courtyard below.

"Lyr," Owen whispered, reading the tension in her twitching tail. He stood, his body stiff. The cold stone floor shocked his bare feet. "Something's up."

"Stay close," he murmured.

Confusion spilled into the room as Owen cracked the door open. Shouts echoed down the stone corridors, followed by a clatter of armor like a tempest of steel and fear.

"By the Ancients ... what now?"

"Make way!" A guard barrelled past, nearly crashing into them. Lyr hissed.

"Ho! What happened?" Owen called after the retreating figure. But the man was swallowed by the chaos.

"Come on." Owen stepped out. Lyr padded silently beside him.

"Prince Owen!" Henrik, breathless and wide-eyed, skidded to a halt before them. "Your Highness, please! Back to your chambers!"

"Tell me what is going on!"

"Orders are orders, my lord. For your safety!"

"Damn my safety!" He needed to know, needed to see with his own eyes the source of this upheaval.

"Please, my lord. I don't want to get in any trouble."

"Fine."

As they turned back, Lyr let out an uneasy growl, her instincts as riled as the air around them. Owen placed a hand on her back, feeling the thrum of her pulse beneath his palm.

"Whatever this is, we'll face it together."

Owen followed Henrick, his half-asleep mind stumbling over itself with each step he took. Was it an invasion? Uprising? There had been whispers ... Unhappy laborers, threats from the Cogsmen who powered the gondolas. Owen had heard them.

"It won't be long, my lord," the footman said as he closed the heavy oak door.

"Will you not even tell me—" Owen started, but he was cut off by the sound of a key turning.

"He's locked us in!" Owen's fingers curled into fists.

Lyr paced, her body tense, emerald eyes darting to the door, then back to Owen. He sank onto the edge of his bed.

Time stretched, thin and taut.

A faint click. A whisper of hinges. The door crept open.

"Nephew," Lady Abria's voice came into the room, as cold and smooth as polished silver. "My poor boy."

"Poor? What do you mean by that? I demand to know what is going on. Why I was locked in this room, why—"

"Owen. Listen to me. Your parents ..." Her eyes wouldn't meet his. "Their gondola ... it fell."

A wave of cold, prickly dread passed over Owen. Fell? His mind reeled. He hadn't even been told they were going out that night.

"Into the Arran gorge," she finished, her gaze finally locking onto his. Pity was painted on her face like a mask.

"Are they hurt?" His voice was a thread, nearly breaking.

"They are ... well, it's not yet known." Lady Abria stepped forward, hand outstretched. He recoiled instinctively from her touch.

"Not yet known?" Anger flared, sending words and thoughts he had never dared to express to the surface. "And is that more convenient for you, aunt? To not find out?"

"Owen!" Her rebuke was sharp as a whip crack.

"Tell me!"

"Enough!" Her command echoed off the walls, leaving a ringing silence. Then her voice softened, sweetened. "We must hope."

Hope. The word felt like betrayal.

"You must rest now." Her silhouette retreated against the candlelight.

As if sleep would come. As if nightmares wouldn't claw at him with the reality that his world might be crumbling.

"Hope," he repeated to Lyr, who blinked in understanding. "The Arran Gorge is hundreds if not thousands of meters deep. There's a fact for you. And she tells us to hope."

Owen lay back onto the bed. Conflicting emotions tumbled within him. No single feeling could gain purchase on him. He felt as though his insides were being torn apart.

And yet he did sleep, for at some point, morning light crept through the barred window, casting a lattice of shadows across the blank walls. He sat upright in bed. Lyr lay curled at his feet, watchful.

The door creaked open. Henrick entered, carrying breakfast on a tray. He wore a sheepish look and avoided his master's gaze. Lady Abria came behind him, something clasped in her hand. A scroll.

"Good morning, nephew."

Owen didn't bother to reply. His fingers burrowed into Lyr's fur.

Henrick left the tray on the nightstand and then hurried out, responding to a subtle signal from Lady Abria.

"I have something that you must see." She unrolled the parchment with a flourish, revealing elegant script.

"Your parents' last wishes," she announced, holding it out for him to see. "They left explicit instructions. In the unfortunate event of their demise ... I am to act as your guardian until you reach the age of majority."

Owen's eyes narrowed. "Their demise? They're not confirmed dead."

"Yes, well." She waved a dismissive hand, her jeweled rings catching the light. "One must be prepared."

"Prepared or presumptuous?"

Her mask slipped. A flash of annoyance appeared, fleeting but unmistakable.

"Show me proof. Proof they're dead and gone."

"Dear boy." Her lips curved into a smile. "You know the gorge is merciless."

"Then search it!" It was the shrill voice of a child, but he couldn't control himself. "Find them!"

"Patience." Lady Abria was clearly enjoying Owen's outburst. She tapped the scroll. "For now, this is all you need to concern yourself with."

"Concern myself? With ink and lies?"

"Reality, nephew." She folded the parchment, her movements precise. "What could very well be your new reality."

"I told you. Show me proof that they are gone."

As if he had been waiting for his cue, the chamber door opened. A wiry, bespectacled man entered.

"Professor Fenlow," Lady Abria announced, waving the man forward as if presenting a prized stallion.

"Your Highness," he bowed low. "I am at a loss for words. It is most lamentable. The gorge is unforgiving. The royal gondola … shattered upon impact. None could survive such a fall."

None. The word was a vice squeezing his chest. Owen turned away, breaths coming fast and shallow.

"See?" Lady Abria's tone was almost gleeful.

"I want to see it with my own eyes."

"Prince Owen," Fenlow interjected, "I've seen the wreckage. My word is—"

"Your word is coin," Owen spat. "Paid for."

"Insolent child." Lady Abria was also losing control herself. Her nostrils flared as she snapped her fingers. Fenlow retreated, bowing obsequiously as he left the room.

"Owen," she began, her voice softening once more. "You must accept—"

"I'll accept nothing."

"Then rage quietly!" She spun on her heel and left him.

Door closing. Footsteps fading. Alone again. Owen's knees buckled, and he sank to the ground. His fingers found the comfort of Lyr's fur. Tears welled, unbidden.

He spent the rest of the day between sleep and wakefulness. Whenever he drifted off, his comforting dreams took catastrophic turns that would awaken him. Then he would lie, tears gathering in his eyes, until sleep took him again. A cycle of pain and escape.

Meanwhile, night fell once again.

It was after midnight when he was awoken by the flutter of wings. Moonlight bathed the room, casting long shadows across the floor. Lyr made soft mewling sounds. There was something perched on the windowsill. Owen sat up. It was a sparrowhawk, head cocked, watching him.

Owen stood and approached the bird, which seemed to have no fear of him. Around its neck hung a silver chain that he recognized as his mother's. From the chain hung a stone the size of Owen's palm. It was smooth, opalescent, almost transparent. Something within it glowed softly, pale red, with what appeared to be the rhythm of a human heart.

"Who sent you?" His voice barely rose above a whisper. He reached out, his fingers trembling.

The bird ducked to allow the chain to slip from his neck. The stone tumbled into Owen's open hand. He turned it over. On its back there was a single word etched into the stone. "Alive."

"It can't be ..." But hope surged, drowning out doubt.

The hawk peered at him and blinked, almost knowingly. Then it turned, bobbed, and took flight.

"Wait ...!"

But the sparrowhawk was gone. Owen breathed, clutching the stone. A beacon, calling him to the deepest recesses of the Arran Gorge.

There was nothing he could do but answer its call. Lyr was watching him intently. She came to him, brushing against his trembling arm. She would be his companion. And yet it was not enough. Neither knew the valleys, their dangers, or how to survive. Without aid, the two of them stood no chance. He needed a guide.

Chapter 4

The Hog's Head

The moon watched as Prince Owen cut across the field that separated the castle from the simple stone cottages that housed its servants.

He was dressed as a page boy, his hair unruly, the stolen uniform loose on his small frame. Shadows clung to him, conspirators in his masquerade.

"Oi," grumbled the sleepy guard at the servants' gate, a whiff of ale on his breath. "Where you off to?"

"Errands for the master," Owen murmured, voice pitched high, unfamiliar. His pulse quickened; he was no actor. The lie sat uneasily on his tongue.

"Night's no time for errands." Suspicion narrowed the guard's eyes.

"Urgent messages wait for no one."

"Go on then, scurry away." The guard waved a dismissive hand and turned back to his post.

Exhaling relief, Owen melded with the night, feet whispering over the path through the woods that led to Arrantown. The path gave way to a wooden platform, polished by age and use, and this brought him to the suspended footbridge where thousands of servants to Arran had come and gone across centuries.

He stepped onto the bridge. It swayed gently, but Owen was not afraid. He could see how well the thick rope was anchored in the stone. He trusted the practicality of the servants more than the abstract diagrams of his engineering professors.

It wasn't long before he was across. The buildings of the town loomed ahead, and Owen picked up speed, plunging into its narrow, labyrinthine streets. Here, the air smelled of woodsmoke and animal fat, of lives lived in the shadow of the crown.

He ducked under laundry lines heavy with damp garments, their shapes ghostly sentinels in the darkness. His heart was still laden with grief but now it was also quickened with hope, with the thrill of escaping the gilded cage that was his birthright. Adventure called to him.

At last, the Hog's Head emerged from the tangle of alleys, its sign creaking on rusty hinges. Dim lanterns cast pools of dubious welcome on the threshold. Owen's stomach tightened. The Hog's Head was the den of the brave and the desperate. According to rumor, it was also the home of thieves, rogues, and adventurers of all kinds.

"Evening," he said to the doorkeeper, nodding the greeting of equals rather than superiors.

"You've come from the castle," the doorkeeper muttered, eyeing Owen's disguise. "Don't make trouble."

"I wouldn't dream of it."

Owen stepped inside. The pub's interior swallowed him whole, a maw alive with raucous laughter and the ringing sound of tankards being slammed against one another.

Owen edged onto a rickety stool at the far end of the bar. He leaned close to the barkeep, his voice a whisper as he tried to hide the refinement in his speech. "Cider, if you will. The sort without a head."

"Soft brew for a soft lad?" the barkeep grunted. Owen nodded, pretending not to notice the sidelong glances.

But it was no use; recognition showed in the eyes of some of Arrantown's less savory residents. Shadows shifted, and one by one they slunk away, dark figures dissolving into the night beyond the pub's grimy windows.

He sipped the cider, feigning indifference. It was then that she caught his eye—a woman with shoulders broad as an ox yoke, absorbed in a game of Dragon's Maze spread across a corner table.

"Watch and learn," she declared. She rolled the dice and her fingers danced nimbly over the carved pieces, guiding a tiny knight across the complicated board. Her opponent, a burly man with a face like thunderclouds, scowled as his dragon met an untimely demise.

"Brains best brawn, Dellen. Now, pay up. Unless you want to go again."

The man, Dellen, grumbled and shook his head as he counted out a stack of coins and pushed them toward the woman. "There you are, Fiona. I still think you cheated."

"You can think that all you want, Dellen. But I won, fair and square. Now get out of here. I'm sure your wife is wondering where you are."

The man slowly gathered the pieces of the game, stowing them under his arm as he made his way to the door.

Owen's gaze lingered on the woman as she deftly collected the coins. But he had seen something that Dellen had not: a second pair of dice that Fiona had let drop from her sleeve unnoticed. A spark of hope kindled in his chest. Perhaps she could be the key to the journey ahead.

"Another round, lad?"

"Ah, no—I'm quite content."

Owen rose. The wooden stool scraped the floor, an echo in the sudden hush of the pub. He squared his shoulders, imagining that the page boy's garb was a knight's armor as he strode toward the woman.

"Excuse me," he began, voice steadier than he felt. "I couldn't help but admire your ... expertise."

She looked up from her winnings. "Expertise?" she echoed, a single brow arched.

"Indeed." Owen's throat tightened. "I seek passage through the valleys of Arran. I need a guide. Someone of your ... talents."

"A game of Dragon's Maze is hardly an endorsement for a guide." She looked doubtfully at his page boy garb. "And what's a page boy after, anyway, in those godforsaken valleys?"

"That's my business."

"Then why should I help you, if you won't even tell me the purpose of the journey?"

"Because," Owen pressed, ignoring the sting of 'boy,' "I am prepared to make it worth your while."

"Money? I've got plenty." She took a leather pouch from her belt and let the coins she had won drop into it, joining the others.

"Then what—"

"Listen, lad. You're too young. Too naive. And frankly, I don't mix with the castle-folk."

Owen looked wildly around him. His plan was unraveling. He took his chance.

"And what if I told you that I saw what you did, just now. You cheated."

Fiona turned to him. Fire burned in her eyes, quickly giving away to amusement.

"So, the pup has a bite. I'll tell you something. Dellen is a low, dirty cheater himself. He's cheated half the people in this place. And he's rich. He may dress like a beggar, but he's the biggest merchant of moonshine in Arrantown. Forgive me if I try to even the score."

Owen stood there, marooned in a sea of rejection. Fiona's dismissal threatened to drown his resolve. But he had ventured too far to retreat now. There must be a way, a lever to move this immovable force before him.

If there was, he couldn't see it. He looked around the pub. The crowd had thinned: the remaining patrons were already half-asleep or drunkenly snoring with their heads on the tables. Not one among them came close to matching Fiona.

Owen nodded. "Goodbye, then." He paid for his cider and left, his quest hanging by a thread.

Chapter 5

A Pact of Silence

Owen slipped through the door, the clamor of the Hog's Head muffling behind him as he stepped into the chill night air. He wrapped his stolen cloak tighter around him, the coarse fabric rough against his chin.

"Wouldn't have pegged him for nobility," murmured the barkeeper, polishing a glass with a dirty rag. His gaze followed the prince's shape through the same grimy windows. Fiona's ears pricked at the words, her interest piqued.

"Wait. Nobility?" Her voice cut across the room.

"Indeed," the owner confirmed, leaning closer as if to share a secret. "Royal blood runs through those veins."

"Royal ..." Fiona repeated, the cogs turning. That was real money. And power. Leverage. She pushed away from the table and strode through the door, determination in her step.

"Hey!" she called out, her voice bouncing off the stone walls. Owen flinched but stopped, half in shadow, half bathed in the pale light. "I might've judged too quickly."

He turned, wary hope flickering in his eyes. "You're interested then?"

"Depends." She eyed him, gauging. "How much are we talking?"

Owen's voice was steady, despite the pounding of his heart. "I have ... resources. Just need a few items from the castle."

"Thievery?" A smirk touched Fiona's lips.

"Let's call it ... borrowing."

"Right." Fiona folded her arms, considering. "Borrowing from your own kin, I take it?"

"Something like that," Owen conceded, swallowing the lump in his throat.

The night had deepened, and the first whispers of dawn were still hours away. A cool mist clung to Arrantown's cobblestones, dampening Owen's boots as he stood rooted, Fiona's impressive bulk looming over him.

"Fine," she said abruptly. "I'll meet you by the old sycamore tree. East side of the castle. Before the cock crows. And you'll tell me no more about this quest than I need to know. Understand?"

Owen nodded, his pulse pounding in his ears. This was it—soon he would be on his way, soon he would find his mother. He watched Fiona's breath curl into the air as she hesitated, regarding him.

"Bring a better cloak. And boots that won't betray you with every step."

"Of course."

"Food for three days," she continued, ticking off on her fingers. "A blade, not for show. And your wits, if you have them about you."

"Understood." He shifted, trying to seem taller, more imposing. But the tremor in his voice betrayed him.

"Three days' food, a real blade ..."

"Lastly," Fiona paused, her gaze fixed on him with unnerving intensity. "No princely airs. Out there, they'll get you killed."

"None," Owen promised, the word a puff of white in the chill.

"Good." Fiona turned. "Don't be late, Your Highness."

The mocking tone of "Your Highness" stung, but Owen stayed silent, watching her merge with the mist.

He had till dawn. To gather, to prepare, to steel himself. The prince exhaled, a lone figure against the backdrop of sleeping homes, and stepped forward into his newly-formed future.

The moon still clung to the horizon, a thin silver crescent fading into the approaching dawn, as Owen slipped once more out of the castle. Over one shoulder was slung a gunny sack, which he tried to keep from jostling, lest its precious contents jangle and give him away. Lyr padded silently beside him, her emerald eyes shimmering in the dim light.

They neared the postern gate. The two guards looked like statues carved from the night itself. Owen set the sack down, gently. He put his hand to the velvet pouch at his belt and began to walk toward the gate. One of the guards spotted him and stepped into his path.

"Your Highness? We have orders to let no one through."

"I am certain you do," Owen replied, his tone cool as he drew a handful of jewels from the pouch. They sparkled like captured stars against his palm. "But I must leave, briefly. And my business requires discretion."

The guard's eyes widened. With a swift move, Owen let the precious stones slide into the guard's eager hand. The clink of gold followed, a sweet melody promising silence.

"See that you forget our passing," Owen said, locking eyes with the man, ensuring the bribe took hold.

"Passing?" The guard pocketed the bribe, feigning ignorance already. "I see no one."

"Good." Owen nodded, satisfaction curling inside.

He picked up the sack and passed with Lyr through the gate.

The series of valleys and peaks beyond them was a dark expanse awaiting the first stroke of dawn. He touched the softly glowing stone, which he had hung around his neck. Somewhere in that expanse was his mother.

Owen's breath misted before him as he crossed the royal bridge. Once on the other side, he skirted the town, picking his way across its rocky outskirts, Lyr's silhouette weaving through the underbrush with fluid grace. At last he found the sycamore tree.

"Should be here," Owen muttered to himself, scanning for Fiona's form.

A rustle to his left, and then a shadow detached itself from the stone. Fiona stood, the sun's first orange rays lighting up her stoic face and mane of auburn hair, the rest of her still cloaked in shadow.

"Took your time."

"Guards needed convincing."

"Let's hope that's all they needed. Did you bring what we spoke of?"

Owen handed her the gunny sack. She crouched down, opened the sack, and looked at its contents. A smile formed on her lips. Then she rose and, finding a suitable stone, lifted it up and dug a shallow hole. She placed the treasure there and replaced the stone after marking it with her dagger.

"There. Now I have to come back in one piece." Fiona turned, gesturing for Owen to follow. Her steps were sure on the dewslick grass.

The prince hurried after her, slipping and sliding and trying not to collide with the sharp rocks that jutted like a giant's broken teeth from the hillside. Their path zigzagged downward, avoiding the series of cliffs that landslides had cut into the slope.

Then, earth betrayed foot. The soft soil gave way beneath him, and Owen felt himself lurch forward. His arms windmilled, seeking purchase on anything solid. He yelped as momentum claimed him, and he went tumbling toward the cliff.

Chapter 6

The Quest Begins

O wen grasped at shrubs, stones, but nothing slowed his runaway descent. The world narrowed to the sensation of falling, his breath trapped in his throat so that he could not even cry out.

"Gotcha," grunted a voice, as iron-like fingers clamped around his ankle. It was Fiona, her grip unyielding, anchoring him to the cliffside.

"Quite the grip," Owen gasped. He was face down on the edge of the bluff with his arms dangling over the side. The taste of grass and dirt filled his mouth, and blood, for his lips were torn. Looking down, he saw the fall that should have claimed his life.

"Didn't take you for a cliff diver."

With a slight heave that made it clear to Owen how little he weighed to her, Fiona hauled him up.

"Thanks," Owen panted once over the edge. He lay on his back for a moment, staring at the brightening sky. The solid ground was like a balm to his rattled nerves.

"Next time, watch your step," Fiona chided, offering him her hand. "It's not a great way to start a quest."

"Understood." He grasped her callused hand. "Sorry."

Owen pulled himself up to a sitting position, wincing as he rubbed at a bruised elbow. "I'm not ..." His gaze fell; he was unable to meet Fiona's eyes. "I'm weak. Untrained."

"Hey." Fiona crouched beside him, her shadow falling across his hunched form. "None of that now."

He glanced up, meeting her gaze.

"Listen," she said, her hand hovering awkwardly before landing on his shoulder with the subtlety of a forge hammer. "You're here, aren't you? With every breath, you get stronger, learn more."

"Sure doesn't feel like it."

"Feeling's got nothing to do with it," Fiona retorted. She stood, brisk, business-like. "We've got a long road ahead. You'll learn or you'll end up food for the crows. I won't sugarcoat it for you."

Owen pushed himself to his feet, dust clinging to his palms. As soon as he had done so, Lyr shimmied up his leg and back, coming to rest on his shoulder and giving him little licks on his ear.

"Hey! Lyr, that tickles." The animal's ministrations embarrassed him. He turned back to his guide. "I don't expect you to."

"Good. Because I won't."

Owen took a deep breath, the cool dawn air filling his lungs, as Fiona stopped briefly to survey the path. She cut a sharp figure against the lightening sky, her gaze scanning the jagged descent before them. Dawn painted the valley in strokes of amber and violet, the world awakening with a hush.

"Once we're clear of this place, I'll teach you to hold that sword you brought. To stand your ground."

"Really?"

"Really." She glanced back at him, one eyebrow arched. "Can't have you tumbling off every cliff we come across."

Owen managed a half-smile, feeling his lip starting to swell. He watched Fiona's boots, the way they found purchase on the uneven ground, and mimicked her steps. The descent demanded focus.

The cliffs loomed large around them, ancient guardians of stone and moss. Shadows clung to their faces, concealing crevices and hollows where anything might lurk—a bandit, a slumbering wolf.

"Keep your eyes peeled," Fiona instructed. "Cover is scarce but necessary. Your first lesson is survival. It's not just about fighting. It's knowing when to hide, when to run."

"Survival," Owen repeated internally, the word settling deep in his chest. He felt its weight, its truth.

"And I wouldn't be wearing that thing around my neck, if I were you. It could get snagged on something. If I were your enemy, it's the first thing I'd grab."

Owen looked down at the stone on its chain. He had taken to calling it "touchstone" in private, for it reminded him of his mother's touch. He felt an urge to explain to Fiona why he was wearing it. Instead, he went to tuck it into his shirt. As he did so, he noticed something.

The glow in the stone had weakened; its pulse had slowed. It reminded him, for all the world, like a small creature dying.

A sharp rap on the chamber door cut through the silence of the room. Lady Abria stirred in bed, her dreams of vast mines and machines rending the earth to spill their precious secrets dissipating. The second knock was more insistent, urgent fingers drumming against the ancient oak.

"Milady," a hushed voice called. It was Elise, her lady-in-waiting, ever dutiful even in the ungodly hours before sunrise.

"Enter."

The door creaked open; candlelight glowed in the dim room. Elise hovered in the doorway, hesitant yet resolute.

"Forgive the intrusion, Milady, but it's Master Owen. He's—" Elise paused.

"Speak," Lady Abria snapped, sitting upright, the remnants of sleep falling suddenly away.

Elise stepped forward, the golden light illuminating concern on her features. "He's just gone, Milady. They say he went toward the eastern slopes."

Lady Abria felt her heart quicken, not with fear, but with a rush akin to anticipation. She slipped from her bed, feet finding her silken slippers with the heel. The king's sister was short. She always wore a heel, even in her nightgown.

"Left?" she repeated, masking her thoughts with practiced indifference. "And who are 'they'?"

"Two guards at the eastern gate. He bribed them."

"Did you retrieve the bribe?" Elise nodded. "Then, why do you wake me with this news?"

"Apologies, Milady. But it appears the prince also took several items from the treasury. Jewels, bracelets. And ..."

"And?"

"Weapons. A sword belonging to your grandfather."

Lady Abria's gaze hardened. Weapons meant more than simple theft or breach of protocol; it spoke of desperation or defiance. Owen had chosen his path.

"Should I call for Sir Galvrey?"

Lady Abria's lips turned slightly upward, a ghost of a smile that never promised warmth. "Not yet."

Elise hesitated, her fingers fidgeting with the hem of her apron. She knew better than to question Lady Abria openly, but her eyes betrayed her concern.

"Very well, my lady." Elise gave a curt nod, lit a second candle that she placed on the table by her mistress's bed, then backed out of the room as silently as she had entered. The door closed, leaving Lady Abria alone with her thoughts.

As the candlelight flickered, Lady Abria sat motionless, contemplating the implications of Owen's flight. He had acted sooner than she had imagined. The threads of possibility spun around her, each one leading to a different tapestry of outcomes. But which one would she weave into reality?

How far will you get, Owen? she thought to herself.

Would he prove himself clever, resourceful? Or would he falter, ensnared by his own folly?

She could send a battalion now to retrieve him, yet she stayed her hand. This was a test—not just of Owen's mettle, but of her own restraint.

"Run, then," she breathed into the night. "Show me your worth."

Chapter 7

Ronat of the Fae

The sun was well past its zenith when they finally reached the forest's edge. Its slanted beams pierced the canopy like golden lances, heralding their arrival into the first valley.

They walked between great trees now—oak trees seven times Owen's age. Lyr was enjoying the new landscape. She scampered up the trunks of the trees, frightening birds into flight. From her position in the canopy, Owen imagined that she had an interesting vantage point.

With each stride, the forest floor gave a soft crunch, a mix of dead leaves and twigs beneath their feet. He glanced up, catching glimpses of a blue sky framed by the towering sentinels of bark and green. Soon the forest of oak gave way to chestnut.

"We'll find respite in these shadows." Fiona stopped and removed her sword. An enormous chestnut stood sentinel among its kin. She motioned toward its base. "Here."

She put down the small pack she was carrying with their provender. "Help me collect tinder for the fire."

Owen nodded. He was drenched with sweat that was rapidly beginning to cool. He copied Fiona, picking up small dry twigs and testing them for dryness.

He felt at home with this woman. It surprised him; he had expected to be afraid of her, and yet there was an impulse in him to share. To let her know him.

"Ever since I was little," Owen began, breaking the silence that had settled between them. His words felt clumsy. "I've wanted to wield magic."

Fiona cast him a sidelong glance. "Magic?"

"Power," he clarified, brushing aside a low-hanging branch. "To protect, to heal. More than swordplay or stealth." A thrush burst from a nearby bush, startled by his admission, wings beating furiously against the quiet.

"Power is earned. Not given. Not even to princes."

Owen sucked his injured lower lip, feeling the sting of truth in her words. He knew his birthright granted him no favor in the wilds.

"Teach me then," he insisted, his voice firmer now. "I want—no, I need to be more than I am."

"Patience, lad. In time. For now, focus on the task at hand. We need to warm you up."

Owen smiled. It was true, his teeth had begun to chatter as the sun disappeared, ray by ray.

The forest seemed to hold its breath as dusk approached, painting shadows upon the earth in strokes of deepening gray. Owen's eyes flicked to the canopy above, watching the last fingers of sunlight dance between leaves.

"Owen," Fiona's voice burst through the stillness. "There's something you need to know about me."

He turned his head. Her eyes, sharp and knowing, seemed to pierce through the gathering gloom. "What's that?" he asked, curiosity piquing.

"I can tell when someone lies." A smirk tugged at the corner of her mouth. "It's a gift. Ever since I was a little girl. That's how I won Dragon's Maze back at the pub."

"Truly?"

"On my life. But keep it close. I don't care for secrets, but this gift won't be worth much if everyone knows about it."

He nodded, savoring the shape and weight of trust newly forged.

As darkness seeped into every nook and cranny of the forest, they sat under the chestnut tree, backs against its gnarled trunk. Above, leaves whispered secrets to the stars. He felt small beneath the vastness of it all, yet strangely fortified by Fiona's presence and confidence.

Owen held the touchstone in his hands. He had begun to feel its pulse, he thought. It was no longer necessary to look at its glow to know its rhythm.

He heard Fiona's breathing become regular and soon he followed her into sleep.

Morning light filtered through the leaves, casting a mosaic of gold and emerald upon Owen's eyelids. He stirred, the unfamiliar hardness of the ground beneath him a stark reminder of his new reality. The scent of roasting meat teased his nose, and he opened his eyes to see Fiona crouched over a small fire.

"Rabbit," she said without looking up. "Caught it at dawn."

"Already?" Owen sat up, brushing off leaves that clung to his hair.

"Sleeping in is for royal beds." She turned the spit. "Out here, daybreak is for the hunt."

He nodded. His muscles ached and his stomach rumbled, betraying his hunger. Fiona laughed and tore a strip off the roast rabbit.

"Thank you," he managed, his voice hoarse from the night's chill. The heat of the meat barely registering against the coldness of his fingers. As he chewed, slow and methodical, he realized another pressing need.

"Uh, where's the privy?" he asked, cheeks coloring.

"Privy?" Fiona laughed again, a harsh bark that made birds take flight. "You're looking at it. Pick a tree."

"A tree?" Discomfort knotted his insides.

"Or dig a hole. Bury your business. Keeps the critters away."

"Right." Owen stood, suddenly conscious of every leaf, every twig. "And—uh—washing?"

"Waterfall's just yonder," she gestured vaguely with her chin. "Can't miss it."

"Thanks." He hesitated, then added, "Fiona?"

"Hmm?"

"Nothing. I'll be back."

"Sure." Her attention returned to the fire. "Take your sword!"

In the solitude of the woods, with only the sounds of nature as company, Owen dug a hole. His hands felt clumsy, the soil cold and damp. This task, so mundane, yet so alien, was humbling.

He thought of the castle privy, porcelain and privacy—a world away. He shook his head. No room for softness here. Not now.

Finishing the necessary, he covered it up, patting down the earth. There, he thought, survival. It's not just about fighting and magic. It's this, too.

Owen followed the sound of cascading water, the murmur growing stronger with each step. His legs were stiff from the unfamiliar bed of earth and leaves, his body longing for the warmth of a good wash.

"Left at the birch," Fiona had said, her voice trailing him like an echo. He had nodded, not quite sure which tree she meant but too proud to ask.

"Come on, Owen," he muttered to himself. "It's just water." But it wasn't just water—it was another reminder of how much he had to learn.

The forest opened up, revealing a break in the canopy where sunlight glistened off a steady stream tumbling over rocks. There it was, the waterfall, a veil of silver churning an otherwise still pool of crystalline water. A sigh escaped him.

"Okay," he breathed, stepping closer. The air was cooler here, mist teasing his skin. He peeled off his tunic, goosebumps peppering his chest.

He reached out, fingers grazing the water's edge. Cold, sharper than expected.

"Gods above," he gasped, flinching back before steeling himself. "You've faced worse, Owen."

He stepped into the pool beneath the falls, breath hitching. The shock of the cold clenched his muscles. He dipped lower, water embracing him fully.

One deep breath and he plunged his head beneath the surface, letting the current wash over him. When he emerged, gasping, laughter bubbled within him.

He stopped laughing, however, when he saw that he was being watched.

Chapter 8

Waterwalk

O wen eyed the wild girl cautiously. She stood barefoot, her long legs and arms brown with many summers. The rest of her was clad in a curious medley of animal pelts and tree bark.

"Peace," she said softly, raising her hands, palms out. Her voice seemed to hum with the life of the forest itself. "I am Ronat."

Owen studied her—the tangled chestnut hair, the freckles dancing across her nose. She did not carry a weapon, nor did any hint of malice glimmer in her clear green eyes, the same color as his own. Hesitantly, he lowered his gaze from the bank where his sword lay.

"Ronat," he echoed back, testing the name on his tongue.

"Come," she beckoned with a tilt of her head, turning towards where Fiona awaited. "Your guide must know I am friend, not foe."

He followed, led by curiosity and an odd, unspoken trust. They approached the camp, where Fiona was now boiling water over the fire in a tin cup. Her gaze fell on them, assessing the situation.

"Who's this?"

"Ronat," Owen replied before the girl could speak. "She means no harm."

Fiona studied Ronat briefly. Then, she nodded once, accepting Owen's judgment.

"Sit," Fiona invited, gesturing towards the still warm fire.

"Thank you," Ronat said, her voice harmonizing with the crackle of burning wood. She reached into a pouch at her waist and produced a handful of berries, deep blue and glistening.

"Gifts of the forest," she smiled, offering them first to Fiona.

"Berries?"

"Safe, I assure you. Nature's bounty for those who wander her paths."

Owen watched as Fiona reluctantly accepted the fruit, still scanning Ronat for deceit. But when no lie presented itself, she popped a berry into her mouth, chewing thoughtfully.

"They're good," Fiona admitted, a rare compliment slipping from her lips.

Owen took a berry, rolling the cool, smooth orb between his fingers before tasting the sweet tang that burst on his tongue. It was a simple act, sharing food that she had foraged, and yet in that gesture was a generosity Owen had never witnessed in his life in the castle.

"Thank you, Ronat."

Fiona was less sentimental. "What do you want with us, Ronat?"

Owen watched the girl as she carefully answered.

"Once," she began, "I knew no other life but that of the Narra. They found me, a babe in the crook of an old willow, and they nurtured me as one of their own."

"The Fae?" Fiona stood up as if bitten. "Do you come alone?"

"I am alone. There is no need for fear. Please, listen to my answer."

The guide's features softened somewhat. She was having the same response as Owen to Ronat's soothing voice. Still, she remained standing.

"Each Narra," Ronat continued, "possesses a gift bestowed by the wilderness. Nochtan, my father, can shift his shape. And Boann, my mother, she speaks to the very soul of the forest."

"Magic ..." Owen could almost see the Fae father's form melting from man to beast and back again. And Boann, her hands outstretched, commanding the growth of trees and vines with a whisper. "What is your gift, Ronat?"

"I'm still discovering that. You see, as seasons changed, so did I. A sense of unbelonging crept into me, a rhythm that broke with the cadence of Narra life."

She tossed another berry into her mouth, chewing slowly.

"Human?" Fiona's curiosity was piqued. She leaned forward, elbows on knees, the firelight glinting off her eyes.

Ronat nodded sadly. "A heart too restless, a spirit too ... dense for the ephemeral existence of my kin."

The admission hung in the air. Owen could feel its gravity. She was an enigma, this girl of the woods—human, yet touched by the Fae.

"I parted ways with Nochtan and Boann. To find my place within this realm, or perhaps between realms."

Between realms. The concept resonated deeply within the prince. As Ronat spoke of her departure from the Narra, his imagination conjured the image of a sister he never knew, a specter of kinship woven into his lineage, only to be snatched away by death before his own birth.

"Owen ..." Fiona's voice brought him back to the present. "It's getting late. We should move on."

He blinked. "Of course."

Ronat stood. For the first time, distress twisted her features. "Please, may I join you? I ... I have felt so alone since I left the Fae."

"I don't see why not," offered Owen. Fiona shot him a look. A Fae child. She didn't like it. Not one bit. But it was the prince's quest. He had paid her to guide him, and Ronat didn't seem to pose much of a threat. She might even be an asset.

"Don't you even want to know where we're going, Ronat?"

"Oh, yes. I suppose I do." Ronat turned to Owen.

"We're going to the bottom of Arran Gorge."

"Arran Gorge?" Ronat giggled. "Oh, you mean Narra Gorge. The Fae call it that. And you call it Arran. How funny."

Owen grinned. He liked Ronat's sense of humor. "And don't you want to know why we're going?"

"Shh!" Fiona looked at him.

"Oh, I'm sorry. That's right. Fiona doesn't want to know. But I'll tell you later, Ronat."

"As long as she doesn't tell me," Fiona growled. "Down to the bottom, back up to the top. Those were our conditions. If I don't know, I don't need to worry about it until we get there. Plus, if you lie to me, I'll know. And after that I'll never be able to trust you. Believe me, it's better this way."

They gathered their sparse belongings, doused the fire, and set forth, feet pressing into the soft forest floor. Ferns unfurled like green scrolls around them, and moss clung to the trees, cloaking the woods in layers of living velvet.

"Watch your step."

Owen heard Fiona and nodded. It was all he could do to stop himself from becoming entranced, lost in the depths of the valley forest, so different from the carefully maintained kingswood. The thickets seemed to breathe as they did, exhaling the musky scent of earth and wood.

Suddenly they came to a place where the trees fanned out to reveal a steep waterfall, a cascade of water crashing against razor-sharp rocks, spray rising into the air.

"Beautiful." Owen breathed out, the sight wrenched something inside him. The roar of the falls sang a song of ancient power so different from the variables in the equations they taught at the academy.

Fiona's brow furrowed as she surveyed the waterfall. "We'll have to find a way around. The two of you stay here."

As if taking offense, Lyr dropped down from one of the trees, the most recent stop on her canopy tour. She didn't want to be forgotten.

"Sorry. The *three* of you."

Lyr sniffed. She followed Fiona into the bush, the two of them moving stealthily, all the more surprising given Fiona's size and power. Owen sat down on a rock to gaze down at the waterfall. He didn't notice Ronat removing her overgarments and wrapping the furs up in a bundle as she stepped into the stream of water.

"Watch this."

Hopping from rock to rock, she moved toward the precipice with a lightness that belied the danger. Strange, melodic words spilled from her lips, hands sketching shapes in the air—fluid, purposeful. A shimmer enveloped her, and she fell forward into the cascade.

"Ronat!"

Owen scrambled to get as close to the edge as he dared. His eyes grew wide with disbelief as he saw the girl walking calmly, vertically down the cascading current. She turned and looked at him, smiling as though she were walking along a sunny path.

As she drew closer to the churning mist, Ronat started to run. At the last moment she jumped, drawing her knees into a cannonball and lifting the bundle of clothing over her head as she aimed herself between the rocks. Owen waited with bated breath. After a few moments Ronat surfaced, unharmed.

"Want to learn?" she called up from the pool, her laughter mingling with the splash of water. "Come, I'll show you!"

Owen took a hesitant step. Doubt gnawed at him. He was afraid. Afraid of falling, of failing yet again.

"Concentrate," Ronat instructed from below, her arms spread wide in invitation. "Listen to the water. Speak to it. Now, repeat after me ..."

Ronat called the incantation up to Owen while he stripped to his underwear. He repeated it, word for word, as he made his way along the rocks, wobbling much more than Ronat had.

With a deep breath, he closed his eyes, envisioning the water coalescing under his feet, forming a walkway as it had done for Ronat. Then he stepped off the last rock.

But the water didn't heed his call.

Instead of standing upon its surface, he plunged downward, the torrent showing no recognition. Panic flared, a bright spark in his chest, as the jagged rocks below rushed up to meet him.

Chapter 9

Lyr's Song

Fiona's heavy boots pressed into the moss, leaving a trail of darker shades in her wake. Lyr's fleet paws left no imprint.

"We can pass through there." Fiona pointed to a thicket where the undergrowth was more sparse and appeared to have been used as a deer run.

Lyr gave a chirp of agreement. She waited for Fiona to decide what to do next. The guide listened carefully. Then came a cry, followed by a splash.

"Owen!"

Fiona and Lyr ran along the deer run to the base of the waterfall, the woman slipping and sliding on the clay-rich soil.

Arriving at the pool, Fiona saw Ronat in the water, yelling strange words up to Owen. She tried to get Ronat's attention, but the roar of the waterfall was too great. She looked up and saw the prince nearing the edge of the waterfall. "No!"

But neither Ronat nor Owen heard her. Fiona watched helplessly as Owen hurtled toward death for the second time in under twenty-four hours. She watched as Ronat's expression changed from one of inviting laughter to deadly seriousness. The girl stood and chanted a series of words Fiona had never heard before.

Owen's body stopped falling and hovered in place, surrounded by the same shimmer that had enveloped Ronat before. Hand over hand, as though she was tugging a rope, she drew him toward the safety of the water's edge. He landed with a gentle bump.

Fiona drew a hand across her brow and let out a sigh of relief.

Owen looked at her, a sheepish smile slowly overtaking his shock.

"Unbelievable," grumbled Fiona. "Both of you. Just dry off and let's go."

"Tell me, Ronat," Owen began as they resumed walking, "how do you know so much about magic? Is it all from living with the Fae?"

"Yes, and practice. Plus a pinch of recklessness. The usual ingredients for magical proficiency."

"Can anyone learn? Even if they're ... not born with it?"

"Magic is fickle; it chooses its vessel carefully. But diligence can coax it out."

"Right." Owen's fingers found the touchstone, feeling its thrumming energy. Despite the close call at the waterfall, he hoped that Ronat would share her knowledge.

He glanced at her. She was eyeing him with a mixture of curiosity and caution.

"Before we press on," Ronat said, as if reading his mind, "one spell."

"But ... you saw. I have no magic."

"Not yet, perhaps. This spell is less complicated. Recite after me ..."

Ronat spoke the words, just as unfamiliar as before. Owen's tongue struggled to form them.

"Enunciate, Owen. The elements are fickle listeners."

He tried again.

"Good. Master it. Speak it with conviction, and it will hold fast."

"Enough dawdling!" Fiona's voice reached back to them. "Daylight is fading, and we've leagues yet to cover."

The spell curled within him. As they walked, he silently mouthed the syllables, committing them to memory. Ronat's instruction echoed in his mind. His hands, at first clumsily, traced the air before him, weaving the spell with cautious optimism.

He was so absorbed in his practice that the subtlety of the world around him had begun to fade—except for one thing.

A snatch of song, ethereal and out of place, pricked at his ears. Fiona seemed oblivious to it. Ronat, who knew the forest better and was more fleet-footed, had gone ahead.

"Do you hear that, Fiona?"

"What?"

"Nothing."

His gaze searched the creeping shadows until it fell upon Lyr. The serpine's slender body followed Fiona's hulking shape along the path.

"Is that you, Lyr?" Owen whispered, stepping closer to the feline creature. She turned toward her, her emerald eyes wide with surprise.

Can you hear me, Owen?

Yes! Yes, I can hear you, Lyr!

This conversation was not taking place with words; Fiona heard nothing of it. But for Owen it was a revelation. His beloved Lyr! She had always seemed to understand him, and here was proof!

How can you hear me, Owen?

Ronat, the girl. She showed me how!

Yes, yes. I know her name. It's about time! I've been trying to talk to you for ages.

Owen's heart was bursting with a mixture of disbelief and triumph. "Ronat! Ronat!"

From farther ahead, she heard him and returned. He explained to her what he was experiencing.

"Exactly," she said, her eyes reflecting pride. "That spell, it's an opening. A bridge between your mind and those who speak without words."

"Animals!"

"What? Where?" Fiona was on alert.

"I've mastered it, the first spell! I can hear Lyr!" The happiness in Owen's voice was unmistakable, a boyish grin spreading across his features. Fiona shook her head. This was not her world. If the children wished to play with spells, that was fine. So long as it didn't lead to anything too serious.

"Can you hear her too, Ronat?"

"No. You need a special bond with a creature for that. But Owen, be careful ..." Ronat cautioned. "Magic is a delicate dance. Pride can lead to—"

"Shh! I'm sorry. Lyr says to be quiet."

The serpine had stopped. Her body was tense, ears swiveling forward. Owen felt the change immediately, the triumph draining away like water through his fingers. Lyr's senses, sharp as razored thorns, had caught something.

Others are near. Lyr's voice vibrated in Owen's mind, urgent and low. *Humans. Not friends.*

Then the sound of a twig snapping invaded the stillness of the clearing.

Chapter 10

Ambushed

"Hide!" Owen grabbed Ronat's arm. They ducked behind a gnarled tree, hearts pounding.

"What's happening?"

"Be scarce, Fiona!" Owen hissed.

Fiona heard him. In the blink of an eye, she had vanished into the shadows of the trees.

Owen held his breath, listening for the trespassers.

Leaves rustled—a signal not of the wind but of stealthy footsteps. Owen flinched. He was afraid, but Lyr's mind-voice was a steady presence in his thoughts, a guiding star.

From all sides.

The shadows around them churned with life as figures detached themselves from the trees and boulders of the forest. Their approach was methodical, a hunter's gait—silent, calculated. Men, cloaked in garments, stepped into the evening light, their faces obscured by hoods.

"Who are you?" Fiona's voice rang out, her hand on the hilt of her sword, ready. "Speak your names or prepare yourselves now for defeat!"

Owen's spellwork seemed a distant memory, his pride swallowed whole by the gravity of the moment. He counted the silhouettes: three, no—five. His grip tightened on his own blade, the leather of the hilt wholly unfamiliar.

"State your business!" he demanded, trying to project strength as Fiona had, a strength he scarcely felt.

No answer came, only the sound of more rustling as the men closed in. There was a flash of steel as a sword was unsheathed, a declaration without words.

"Ronat," Owen thought desperately, seeking her guidance. "What do we—"

"Fight smart," she replied through gritted teeth, brandishing her own sword. "Back to back. Protect each other. They have the advantage of numbers."

She edged closer to him, her stance defiant yet wary.

The first assailant lunged, a blur of motion aimed at Fiona. She parried, metal clashing, sparks dancing briefly in the air. Owen took a step forward, only to be pushed rudely back by Fiona.

"Get back, Owen!"

She had a second attacker on her now. One gave a cry of pain as he fell forward. Ronat stood behind, her blade crimson with the attacker's blood. Fiona had recovered and knocked the other man over the head with the butt of her sword, leaving him unconscious.

Owen watched Ronat and Fiona fight from inside the hollow where Fiona had pushed him. From beneath the adrenaline bubbled a sense of shame. He was no fighter; he couldn't even protect himself.

Now's no time for shame, Owen.

I feel so useless, Lyr.

You are not!

Owen felt grateful for Lyr, and for Ronat's spell. He saw the wilding and Fiona dispatching the attackers. Soon, two lay on the ground, one dead and one knocked unconscious. A third had fled; Fiona had the blade of her sword pressed against the neck of the fourth.

"Please!" he cried. "Have mercy! This was as much an ambush for me as it was for you!"

"What do you mean?" Fiona pressed the blade harder against the man's throat. "Be quick!"

"I—I am Cathal, of Lady Abria's royal guard." The man's helmet fell to the ground as he pulled it off, revealing a face etched with concern. "I thought we came for the boy's rescue, not his doom."

"Rescue?" Fiona echoed, easing the pressure on her sword by a fraction.

"Swear it on your life."

"Upon my honor and soul," Cathal pleaded, his voice cracking. "I was misled, used as a pawn."

"Your honor is worth as much as a traitor's promise."

Still, Fiona withdrew her sword. As the guard Cathal scrambled to sit, she searched his face, seeking the lie. A royal guard? Could this be another trick?

"Prove it," she said at last.

Fiona's eyes held Cathal's. His pulse fluttered under the skin of his throat like a trapped bird. There was fear in every line of his face.

"Please. It's not what you think." A bead of sweat trickled down his temple. "Lady Abria ... she moves against the boy."

"Against Owen?"

"Y-yes! She seeks the throne, sees him as an obstacle."

"An obstacle ..." Fiona's thoughts churned. Lady Abria, the "viper in silk," as the Arranfolk called her. Could she have orchestrated this? It made a cruel sort of sense.

"Abria will stop at nothing," Cathal continued. "I swear it."

Owen had emerged from his hiding place before Fiona spared Cathal. He turned to the guard now.

"If she thinks I'm such an obstacle, then why is it a surprise that she would want me dead?"

"Well, because ... You are blood. Family."

Fiona stared at Cathal. There was no trace of subterfuge on his face. *How could a royal guard, a warrior, be so naive?* she wondered. And yet his innocence was touching.

"Stand, Cathal. Go back the way you came and say nothing of this meeting. Tell your captain that your friends got lost. And take this one with you." Fiona nudged the unconscious guard with her boot.

"No."

"What's that? Did I not just spare your life?"

"I ... I cannot. I will not. Now that I know her motives, I won't go back into rank and file for Lady Abria."

"Then what do you suggest?"

"Let me join you. Despite what you saw back there, I can fight. I can protect the boy."

"How do we know this isn't a trick? Maybe you were instructed to make this case if you were caught."

"Lady Abria doesn't know anything about those with whom Prince Owen travels."

Fiona paused. Cathal was telling the truth. Still, she was having difficulty concentrating on the task of interrogating the guard. Why? When the answer came, she blushed. Owen saw the color climb into her cheeks and did a double take. Fiona? Blushing?

"I vote to bring him with us," he said. "He can help us should we run into any more trouble. Ronat?"

"I agree."

I agree, too.

"Lyr agrees. That's three against one."

Fiona sighed. She sheathed her sword and helped Cathal to his feet. He was small, but strong. She felt it in his grip. "Come on. Let's go find a place to rest."

As they collected themselves and found the path once more, Owen and Lyr fell behind the others. The prince found himself in fervent conversation with the serpine. Her lithe form had allowed her more access to the castle than Owen had realized. He was quiet now as she explained to him the true nature of the reality he had once accepted without question.

Chapter 11

Arran Ingenuity

The chamber was a cold bloom of steel and glass, as angular and precise as the woman who stood at its heart. Lady Abria, her gaze fixed upon the touchstone, allowed a thin smile to curve her lips.

"Quite the clever ruse, isn't it?" she murmured, fingers hovering but never touching the stone's smooth surface. The air thrummed with latent power, an invisible force that felt more mechanical than mystical.

Sir Galvrey, head of royal intelligence lurked behind her, eagerly seeking any shred of forbidden information.

Lady Abria continued, imagining her voice a scalpel slicing through ignorance, "They think their Fae magic so grand, so superior. But what is magic without understanding? Without control?" She tapped a rhythm against her leg, a Morse code of disdain.

"Magic," she scoffed, turning the touchstone over with a pair of tweezers, "is just science we have yet to explain. And this—" Her eyes shone like twin shards of obsidian. "This is magnetic resonance, a homing beacon of sorts. Crafted not with wands and spells, but with intellect and precision."

The old spymaster held his breath, trapped between awe and terror. Magnetism—a force invisible, yet undeniably real. It was a concept he had struggled to grasp, one that seemed to live at the edges of sorcery and scholarship alike.

"See," Lady Abria said, lifting a slender device that buzzed softly, reacting to the touchstone's presence, "it seeks its counterpart, driven by forces that Fae enchantments could never hope to harness. They bind their will to the elements, to chance. We," she paused, her gaze hardening, "we bind the elements to our will. To the certainty of science."

With a flick of her wrist, the touchstone levitated, encased in an invisible grip stronger than any physical chain. Lady Abria's mouth twisted smugly as she watched it spin, slowly at first, then gaining momentum.

"Let them prattle on about the 'old ways' and the 'ancient arts.' In the end, it is the human mind, our relentless pursuit of knowledge, that will prevail."

The stone spun faster, becoming a blur. The air crackled, the chamber's sterility yielding to a storm of unseen energy.

"Magic," Lady Abria whispered, almost lovingly, to the whirlwind she had conjured, "is nothing compared to the might of human ingenuity."

And in the shadowed archway, the spymaster shuddered, as much from the chill of the room as from the chill in his mistress's soul. He watched as Lady Abria let the stone drop before moving toward a console of arcane machinery. The brass and copper danced with light, screens aglow with the lifeforce of captured stars. Her pale fingers caressed the controls, coaxing whispers from the mechanisms.

"Show me," her sharp voice commanded. The main screen flickered, revealing a map etched in pulsing, luminescent lines. A dot blinked steadily amidst the web of pathways—the touchstone, and closer than it should be to the lip of Arran Gorge and the sister-in-law who should have been killed instantly.

"Impossible." The guards were elite, handpicked for their ruthlessness, their loyalty to her cause. And still, this boy eluded them. Something had gone wrong. With every blink of that accursed dot, her fury mounted.

"Curse his tenacity!" The words left her lips like venom. She slammed a fist on the console; the impact resonated through the chamber, startling the head of intelligence.

Owen's defiance was a blemish on the perfect canvas of her plan. He was nothing more than a gnat, yet he dared to challenge her?

She leaned closer, eyes locked on the screen. The pulse of the touchstone beat like a taunt. It was out there—moving, mocking, escaping. They were supposed to be immobilized, trapped by her ingenious snare, not ... advancing.

"By the gears and cogs, they will not best me!"

The console hummed, a constant reminder of her own brilliance. Yet here she was, thwarted by a boy with nothing but a fancy pussycat and a washed-up adventurer.

"Focus, Abria. Owen is but a variable in your equation. Solve him." Her mind whirred into gear, calculations forming amidst the storm of emotions. Anger was a tool, but logic—logic was the key.

Her gaze remained fixed on the glowing blip. The chase wasn't over. She would recalibrate, respond, and reclaim what was hers. Owen would learn the harsh taste of defeat, and Lady Abria would be the one to spoon-feed it to him. Even if it meant murder.

Chapter 12

A Revelation

O wen's breath formed a white cloud that hung in the cold morning air. They were now deep in the second valley. It wouldn't be long before they crossed the next river and ascended the opposite side of the ravine. Then they would descend the gorge.

He could see the gondola tower perched on the crest of that hill, high above them. The tower looked strange without its cabling—a relic intended for purposes now long forgotten. Owen could see Arran's culture as if from the perspective of a futureling. Their ways (*my ways*, he reconsidered), their incessant demand for more energy, more power, would be met with confusion and disbelief. Or at least that's what he hoped.

The chill of the morning was in stark contrast to the heat of betrayal burning in his chest. The revelation echoed in his mind. He saw Lady Abria's face, twisted into a murderous snarl, an image haunting the edges of his vision.

"Murder," he whispered. "My murder." He'd bristled under her scornful gaze often enough, but the intent to kill? That was a bridge too far, one he'd never thought she would cross.

"Owen." Fiona's voice startled him. He had thought he was alone. "Can we talk?"

"Alright." His nod was a jerky marionette's motion. Trust had become a treacherous path, one he was wary to walk again.

Fiona looked at him, seeming to divine his thoughts. "I know you must be in shock. There's little I can say that might take the bitterness from this betrayal. It's a terrible thing. Still, first we were three. Now we are five."

"What do you mean?"

"When we began, I told you not to tell me anything more than I needed to know. I made the request out of selfish interest. I'm sorry, Owen, but I'm not stupid. Before we left, I heard rumors of your parents' accident. I presume we are going to find them."

"Her. To find *her*. Not them."

"I see. And what makes you think Lady Abria and her men haven't reached the gondola already?"

"They don't know she's alive."

"How do you know she's alive?"

Owen held up the touchstone. "After I learned of their accident, I was given this." He handed it to Fiona, who turned it over in her hands.

"Alive," she read. "Owen, who gave you this?"

"A ... a bird. A sparrowhawk, I think."

"Oh, Owen. More magic, I suppose." Fiona shook her head. She wore a different expression now than any of those Owen had seen before. It reminded him of his mother, the queen.

Cathal stepped forward, bowing his head slightly. "I'm sorry for eavesdropping. It wasn't my intention. But I can't ignore what I overheard. From what I heard before I left Arrantown, I believe the young prince is right."

"About what?"

"I believe his mother may be alive. And there is some ... indication that Lady Abria thinks so as well, though she may not be certain."

"Your knowledge is welcome, Cathal," Owen said. He met Fiona's eyes briefly and wasn't sure what he found there. A silent promise of protection, yes. But something more.

Cathal nodded and turned back to finish striking camp. Fiona watched him move. He was lithe, with such grace. Again, Fiona felt tricked. The man reminded her of Lyr, and yet since he had appeared, she could not stop thinking of him.

She turned back to Owen. There was a dejected look on his face. She sat beside him and put her arm on his shoulder. "So, we have to get there first."

Owen looked at her, his face beaming with gratitude.

The glint of steel flashed through the air, a silver arc against the dusk. Fiona's sword met Cathal's with a ringing clash that echoed through the forest clearing. They moved in a dance of deadly grace, their bodies speaking a language of thrusts and parries Owen could barely comprehend.

"Watch the footwork," Cathal grunted, advancing with a series of precise strikes that Fiona deftly countered.

"You watch mine."

Owen stood to the side, his fingers curling and uncurling at his sides. His eyes traced their movements, each step another reminder of his own ineptitude.

A flutter of movement caught his eye. Ronat, her hands weaving through the air, her lips moving in silent incantation. Wisps of ethereal light gathered around her, responding to an unseen call only she could hear. Power rippled from her, an invisible tide that Owen could never hope to harness.

Something wrong, Owen? Lyr peered at him from beneath a hood of autumn leaves. She too had been busy looking for grubs.

Nothing.

But it was a lie. His gaze drifted back to the sparring duo. Ronat alone in the dell, weaving magic. Alone amidst allies. Owen's helplessness agonized him.

"Focus!" Cathal barked suddenly, and Fiona lunged, forcing him back.

"Easy for you," Owen muttered under his breath, the touchstone against his chest. The stone seemed colder than before. He looked down at it. Still glowing, but the light faltered. Then it went out.

Panic surged within him. He gasped. Then the light rekindled. The glow of the touchstone continued.

"Owen? What is it?" Fiona and Cathal stopped sparring. They looked with concern toward Owen.

"It's alright, now. The touchstone ..." He rose, meaning to show them, but his feet caught on a root that seemed to spring from the earth to that purpose. He stumbled, the world tilting wildly.

"Careful!" Ronat's warning came too late.

He fell, gasping again as he felt the rocky ground scrape against his skin. His knee throbbed, a bloom of pain. He blinked, trying to dispel the disorientation he felt, the tears of pain gathering at his eyes.

"Here, let me."

Ronat knelt beside him. Her fingers were deft as she unfolded a piece of cloth, its edges frayed by time. She pressed it gently against his wound. The fabric was embroidered with an intricate, alternating pattern of silver and blue. A pattern unmistakably noble, unmistakably familiar.

"Where did you get this?" Owen asked, wincing as the fabric dabbed at the raw edges of his wound.

"Found with me," Ronat answered, her attention on staunching the blood. "When I was brought to the Narra as a babe."

Owen reeled with more than pain. Fragments of memory flitted at the edge of his consciousness, elusive and taunting. The very pattern on the cloth seemed to pulse with significance.

His eyes locked onto the cloth and then to Ronat's face.

"Brought by whom?"

"Does it matter?" Her hands stilled, and she looked up at him. "I never knew my kin."

A shiver ran down Owen's spine. He knew, with a sudden jarring clarity, that the pattern on the cloth was the same as the bed linen that had clothed his bed since childhood, the napkins used to dab at the corner of royal mouths, and the tapestries that had graced the halls of Arran castle. The truth clawed its way up his throat.

"Emyr ..." he whispered. His sister's name, a prayer their mother had uttered each night with him until he was twelve years old.

Ronat was still looking at him, brows knitted. "Why do you speak that name?"

"Because ..." Owen's breath caught. "It's yours."

Her hands fell away from his knee, the bloodied cloth dropping between them.

"Impossible." But there was a tremor in her voice, a crack in the certainty of her world.

"Look at me, Ronat." He reached for her, his fingers brushing the sleeve of her tunic. "The House of Arran ... our sigil is woven into that cloth. You are Emyr, my sister, stolen from us when still at our mother's breast."

"Stolen? And who was the thief?"

"I meant it figuratively. Or I thought I did. I was always told you died in infancy."

Doubt clouded Ronat's eyes. Yet, beneath it, something else—a recognition at odds with her words. She touched her own cheek, as if trying to trace the lineage through her flesh. Owen's hand reached out, as well, trembling. He brought his fingertips to her other cheek.

"Sister."

She looked at him, as if for the first time, scanning his light green eyes, the sparse freckles on his nose, the shape of his mouth. And she saw herself.

"Brother," she returned, at last, the word unfamiliar, yet fitting perfectly into the space between them.

Chapter 13

The Weight of Kinship

Owen watched Ronat's face, awash in confusion and awe. Questions danced in her eyes. "Is it true then?" she whispered, voice trembling like a leaf in the wind. "We share more than this quest. We share blood?"

Her words hung suspended in the air, as if time itself had paused to listen. Owen's heart was a tumult of feelings—longing, regret, and uncertainty. The tension between them was palpable, each word charged with significance. He nodded slowly, unable to find the right words to express what he was feeling. "Yes, Ronat. Or should I ... may I call you Emyr?"

"Emyr," she repeated, holding the name inside her. She finally shook her head, a frown like a shadow across her features. "No ... I don't think I'm ready."

Owen nodded. He understood her hesitation. He himself hadn't always liked his name, which bound him to the House of Arran. But his mother had chosen it, the name of one of her favorite uncles. Owen thought of Queen Deirdre now, alone, trapped amid the wreckage of the gondola, cold and afraid. How long could she survive like that? Had she managed to find food and shelter? He promised himself that he would find time to tell Ronat about their mother before they rescued her.

The crackle of a fire drew their attention away. The scent of roasted meat wafted on the breeze, gamy and rich. Cathal stood by the flames, his hands deftly working to skin a second rabbit he'd caught earlier. The first was spitted and dripping fat as it roasted over the fire.

"Seems your talents extend beyond the sword," Owen remarked as they approached the makeshift hearth.

Cathal looked up, a grin spreading across his creased, handsome face. "One cannot live on steel alone, my prince."

Crouched beside him, Fiona poked at the fire, coaxing the flames higher. She glanced up, her gaze sharp, always searching for truth. "What brings you two over? Finally tired of secrets and shadows?"

"Actually," Owen started, "we've discovered something––"

Truly remarkable," Ronat finished for him, her voice steadier now. "Owen is ... my brother."

"Brother?" Fiona's eyebrows shot up and her jaw dropped, but her subsequent smile was genuine. "How ... how can you be sure?"

Excitedly, the siblings filled the guide and the former guard in, their words tumbling forth, telling of rumors and noble patterns. "A napkin ...!" Fiona marveled.

Cathal rose to his feet. "Congratulations are in order, then," he said, clapping Owen and Ronat on their shoulders. "Your family grows, even in these dark times."

Their laughter mingled with the crackling of the fire, a moment of light and lightness amidst the encroaching darkness of their weighty journey.

As their laughter died down, a rustle from the brush announced Lyr's return. The serpine padded softly into the campsite, her eyes narrowing at the sight of the roasting rabbit.

What a stench. Lyr's voice echoed in Owen's mind, tinged with distaste. *Death cooked over an open flame.*

Owen winced, sharing a glance with Ronat. "It's just food, Lyr. I happen to know that you would eat a rabbit without a second thought, if you could catch one."

I can catch a rabbit! Lyr countered, settling beside them with an air of resignation. *But I don't need to kill it twice, as you do with your barbaric fire ritual.*

"Hm ... Guess what we found out?" Owen said aloud, eager to change the subject and cover the sounds of his own rumbling belly, beckoned by the tasty-smelling meat. He gestured between himself and Ronat. "We're kin—brother and sister."

Known to me. Your scents entwined long before your minds accepted it.

Owen goggled. "Then why didn't you ...? Oh, never mind. Anything useful from your scout?"

Useful? A ripple of excitement thrummed through the mental link. *The gondola tower, broken cable dangling into the Gorge. Follow it, and you find her—the Queen.*

"Mother?" Owen's heart surged. He turned to the others. "Lyr found a way! We can trace the cable to Mother!"

The group gathered around, absorbing the revelation. Plans formed, strategies discussed. Eyes alight with purpose.

Beside him, Ronat was silent. Her gaze distant, thoughts churning. Doubt shrouded her, dark and heavy as the furs she wore. Reunion loomed, yet fear clung to her spirit, an unwelcome cloak.

"Emy—I mean, Ronat?" Owen reached out, seeking her hand. "We'll be together again—all of us."

"Will we?" Her voice was soft, barely audible above the crackle of the fire. Embers glowed beneath the rabbit, casting a warm halo on their faces. Ronat hesitated before accepting the skewered meat from Cathal's outstretched hand. The scent mingled with memories, forest and fern––the Narra Fae's sanctuary. Her stomach twisted—not in hunger, but with conflict.

"Thank you, Cathal." The words felt foreign, Arran courtesy clashing with ingrained Narra etiquette. How could they understand that, where she came from, thanks were given only after the meal?

Owen watched her, his expression threaded with concern. Fiona chewed thoughtfully, eyes narrowing on Ronat's troubled face. She had a knack for sensing lies, but here sat only truth––a soul divided.

"Ronat," she whispered to herself. The name bound her to Nochtan and Boann, guardians of green boughs and laughing brooks. It was guidance, love, safety—everything she knew, despite the frequent absence of her adoptive parents and their appetite for trickery. "Emyr," she said next, tasting the name like a curious berry picked from an unknown bush. It was hers too, wasn't it? But it echoed oddly, resonating with a heritage she'd been taught to distrust.

"Both are you," Owen said softly, catching the names as they lingered in the air.

"Two halves of one," Fiona added. A rogue's wisdom, recognizing duality as strength. "Now, we should sleep. I know everyone is excited, but tomorrow will be a long day."

The night deepened, stars emerging like pinpricks through velvet. Shadows stretched, beckoning sleep. Lyr curled up beside Owen, their minds still buzzing with silent conversation. Cathal had neither cape nor sleeping bag. Fiona reluctantly made room for him in hers, her scowl betraying a reluctant bond.

Ronat retreated to her own space, a patch of thatch she'd woven with practiced hands. Furs enveloped her like an embrace from a life she feared losing touch with. Eyes closed, she listened to the symphony of the woods below the plateau, seeking solace in its familiar cadences.

Around her, the others settled into slumber. Breath by breath, the camp's rhythm slowed, yet Ronat's heart raced against the quiet. Tomorrow held answers, reunions, truths. Tonight, she clung to her names, her worlds, and the hope nestled within their syllables.

Ronat stirred. The world around her lay cloaked in the pre-dawn blue, still and unsuspecting. Her heart was filled with unrest; the quiet around her was an illusion. She had to leave. Now.

She rose, her movements soundless as her companions breathed in deep slumber. Even Lyr seemed lost in dreams.

Her burden was light with her few belongings. With each item tucked into her furs or hung from her belt, her resolve tightened. She couldn't face what dawn would bring, not with the weight of her new kinship pressing down on her.

A glance at Owen. His chest rose and fell, peaceful. Guilt gnawed at her. But this was bigger than blood bonds. It was about survival, identity. She couldn't lose herself to the quest. Not to the Arrans, nor their ways.

The thatch crunched softly beneath her boots as she turned away. One step, then another. The valley below beckoned, a gateway back to the Narra Fae, back to Nochtan and Boann.

Where do you wander? The voice was not a sound but a sensation, filling her mind with sudden warmth.

Lyr.

The animal's eyes glinted, reflecting the first hint of dawn. Ronat's breath caught. She hadn't expected Lyr to wake, to reach out with that invisible thread that connected her to Owen … and, apparently, to her.

"Below," she whispered, unsure how much to reveal.

Alone? Lyr's presence in her mind was curious, probing.

"Alone," she confirmed, her heart sinking. Betrayal, even to a creature of few words, stung sharp and true.

Paths fork and wind. Yours is unclear.

"Perhaps." Ronat's defiance wavered. She couldn't explain the pull of Nochtan and Boann's itinerant love, a love that grew in every shoot of grass, every flowering lily, every curious tree root. She didn't have the words to describe how it warred with what she now understood to be the blood of the Arrans flowing through her veins.

"Goodbye, Lyr," she said in her heart, hoping the serpine would understand.

Goodbye, Ronat. Goodbye, Emyr, came the soft echo, a farewell to all she was, all she might yet become.

Chapter 14

The Earth Shakes

Ronat slipped away, her footsteps hushed against the soft earth. She glanced back just once—Owen's slumbering form, Fiona's steady breathing, her slab of an arm slung across the gentle rise and fall of Cathal's chest, and Lyr's silver tail flicking as she watched the girl, an animal's ancient wisdom staying any telepathic warning it might give to Owen.

The trail wound like a serpent beneath her fur-clad feet, familiar yet foreboding in the cloak of night. Trees clustered tight, their branches interlocking above, creating tunnels of leaf and bark. Ronat's heart beat rapidly. She knew the risks of traveling alone, the dangers that crept within the unseen spaces of the woods.

With a deep breath, she summoned her magic, whispering words taught by Boann. Ronat's fingers danced through the air, tracing symbols only she could see. Sparks ignited at her fingertips, and from the depths of the underbrush, fireflies emerged. They swirled around her, a living constellation that painted the path with light.

Ronat moved with renewed purpose. Her eyes scanned every inch of ground, every leaf and twig. Her ears tuned to the subtlest of sounds—the rustle of a nocturnal creature, the distant call of a night bird. Magic flowed through her veins, a connection to the land that grounded her, that reminded her of who she was.

She knew the sun would soon crest the horizon, its first rays piercing the veil of night. Soon, her companions would stir and awaken to discover her treacherous absence. Her heart ached to think of it.

Suddenly, the earth shook. A loud crack, followed by a rumble that thundered through the vale, clawing at Ronat's senses. Another blast, then another, shattering the silence of dawn like a hammer on glass. She froze, heart slamming against her chest. Far, far above her, perched on the distant ridge, the stone gondola tower spat fire and smoke into the graying sky.

Explosions multiplied, each more violent than the last. The ground vibrated with fury. Her eyes turned to where the small plateau clung to the hillside. There, Owen, Fiona, Cathal, and Lyr remained, in the path of danger.

Boulders closer to the ridge, free from their ancient beds, began an unstoppable descent. They bounded down the slope, pulverizing everything in their path.

"Abria," she hissed through gritted teeth, the name a venomous curse. Her unknown aunt's malice and hunger for power had no bounds. Ronat's breaths came fast, her mind a whirlwind. The image of her friends—her family—crushed beneath the mountain's wrath ignited a blaze within her. She had to get to them, warn them.

But the path upward was a gauntlet. Pebbles skipped past, harbingers of the larger death that followed their trail. To climb would be to step into the maw of destruction itself. Her muscles tensed, ready to sprint, to defy the cascading peril—but fear coiled tight around her resolve, flashing warnings of crushed bones and final breaths.

Ronat's gaze darted between the ascending danger and the sanctuary of the valley below. Time thinned, every second a precious drop of opportunity slipping through her fingers. The choice lay stark before her: venture into the jaws of chaos or abandon those she loved to a grim fate.

The Narra girl reached out with her senses, imploring the wisdom of the woods to guide her. Her fingers brushed against the rough pine bark, the trees standing sentinel around her—a silent congregation of witnesses to her desperation.

"Boann's grace," she murmured, a plea to the air and earth that cradled her. The knowledge she sought was elusive, a melody half-remembered, notes rising and falling just beyond her grasp. She closed her eyes, straining to capture the teachings Boann had given her when Ronat was still unsteady on her legs.

The spell ... to speak with rocks, to coax them from their destructive path. It flickered at the edges of her memory. Ronat breathed deep, willing the incantation to surface, to take form in her consciousness.

"Guide the stone, bend its path, heed my voice ..." The words began to coalesce, a fragile song against the thunder of tumbling rock and splintering timber.

But with each syllable that came into focus, so too did the shadow of another, darker chant—one that could turn the mountain's heart to molten fury. The two spells twined like serpents, one promising salvation, the other devastation. The lines between them blurred dangerously, and Ronat knew the peril of invoking the wrong spell.

She needed precision in the weaving of her will into the fabric of the world. A slip, a falter, and the very stones she aimed to redirect could become a river of fire, consuming all in its path—including those she wished to protect.

Sweat beaded on her brow as Ronat steadied her breath. She would have to reach deep, to find the clarity amidst chaos. Her mind grasped at the ragged edges of memory. There it was—the incantation—etched in the recesses of her thoughts.

"Steadfast stone, bend to my plea!"

She surged up the hill, each stride imploring the very bones of the land. The ground shook with anger or fear; even the earth seemed uncertain beneath the relentless bombardment from above.

"Shift your course, yield to me!" She was breathless now, and yet her voice grew stronger, finding its power.

Boulders rumbled down around her, but Ronat's spell wove an invisible shield. Stones diverged, skirting her path as if repelled by an unseen force. She ducked under a massive rock that veered away at the last moment, sparing her from being crushed.

"Harmony, not havoc," she gasped. "Refuge, not ruin!"

The mountain responded to her call, its fury momentarily tamed. Ronat darted and weaved, her feet barely touching the path as she climbed higher, ever closer to her friends, to the discovery of whether they lived or had perished.

Chapter 15

Boulder Run

With a roar, the earth shook. Owen stumbled, his heart racing, as he tried to keep his footing on the shaking ground. Lyr clung tightly to him; Fiona and Cathal called to him as rock broke away from the hillside and smashed through their camp.

Dust clouded the air, stinging his eyes and filling his nostrils with the acrid smell of explosives. This was no earthquake.

"Ronat!" He spotted his sister running up the path. He could see her mouth moving, but the words were drowned out by the deafening roar of the landslide.

But then, suddenly, it all changed. The earth had not ceased its trembling and the dust still swirled, but the rocks seemed to cut a wide path around the plateau. Ronat stood in front of Owen, her hand outstretched as though in defiance of the havoc around them.

Owen could hardly believe what he was seeing. His sister had controlled the very rock itself, bringing the landslide to a halt with nothing but the power of her spells.

"Move!" Ronat's voice cut through the commotion.

Fiona was already on her feet, her massive frame a shield as she pulled Owen up. Cathal's sword was out, glinting, useless against the stone onslaught but ready for human threats.

"Can't believe ..." Owen gasped, his mind's eye seeing only the gorge on the other side of the ridge. The deep valley where gears and steam, the lifeblood of the Arran kingdom, were tended to by hundreds of engineers, laborers, and their families.

"Abria's madness knows no bounds," Ronat seethed, vines curling around her fists unconsciously, a reflex of her nature-whispering talents. "We have to move, Owen. I can't hold the stone forever." She scanned the hill, seeking a path through the destruction.

They scrambled over rocks, each step perilous as the ridge heaved. The ground beneath Owen's boots betrayed him, loose stones sending him skidding. Fiona's hand, firm and sure, caught his arm, steadying him. Cathal darted ahead, small and nimble, finding footholds where none seemed to exist.

"Engineering works ..." Owen panted. "People ..."

"Survival comes first!" Fiona shouted back.

"Ridge top," Ronat pointed upward. "We stop the explosions."

They climbed. Explosions echoed. Each detonation threatened to bury them, to crush the Arran residents of the Narra Gorge. They would reach the top. They had to.

The hillside trembled, a growl rippling through the earth. Ronat's eyes widened as the shadow loomed—a massive boulder, thundering down upon them with merciless speed. She thrust out her hands, murmuring incantations, but the stone monolith defied her command. It was too immense, moving too fast.

"Owen!" she screamed. But the boulder was already upon them.

Owen's heart lurched. Time slowed. He watched in horror as the juggernaut of rock severed their group. Fiona and Cathal, mere silhouettes now, were flung to one side. Lyr, thrown from her embrace of him, was caught in the direct path. The prince's cry was a blade, sharp and desperate.

"LYR!"

He surged forward, every fiber straining toward the chaos, toward his animal friend. Dust clouded his vision; the roar of destruction filled his ears.

"Owen, no!" Ronat grabbed him, her slender fingers belying a grip of iron. "It's too late!"

He fought against her, wild-eyed. "I can feel her! She's in pain!"

But Ronat held fast, pulling him back as the world steadied and the last of the rocks settled. Silence fell like a shroud.

"Listen," Ronat whispered.

The echoes of their panting breaths were joined by another sound—the metallic scrape of boots on stone, the creak of ropes. Men descended from the ridge, shadows turning solid, materializing from the dust.

"Abria's men …" Owen's voice was hollow, his thoughts still with Lyr. Ronat's face mirrored his distress, her expression bearing the added weight of sorrowful resolution.

"Stay close," she murmured, her eyes scanning for any escape route. To their left, a copse of gnarled trees promised cover. "This way," she hissed, tugging at Owen's sleeve.

Owen stumbled after her. He could hear Lyr's voice within him, catches of song lost in a tempest. They came and went, growing fainter. Instinctively, he grasped the touchstone around his neck, reassuring himself that it was still glowing, albeit weakly. Lyr had to be alive as well. His heart clawed at the possibility.

"Keep low," Ronat instructed, as they ducked under a low-hanging branch. The rustling of leaves and snapping twigs blended with muffled shouts and heavy breathing. The sounds of pursuit.

"Can you feel it?" Owen whispered between labored breaths, not daring to raise his voice. "Lyr's essence?"

Ronat glanced back at him, her expression unreadable. "We can't focus on that now, brother. We survive first."

"Survival is nothing without her." He choked on the words, the bond between him and the serpine was unlike anything he had ever known.

"Then we find them all." Ronat's tone was resolute. "Fiona, Cathal, and Lyr."

They pressed on, the terrain steepening. Behind them, branches cracked in the hands of their pursuers, a relentless reminder of the danger at their heels.

"Trust me, Owen. Trust that I can lead us to safety—and to them."

Owen nodded, grasping onto that sliver of hope as if it were a lifeline. With Ronat's conviction guiding them, they moved into the forest, toward the echoes of those they had lost.

Leaves crunched underfoot, betraying their haste. One of Abria's men, hearing them, shouted to the others to hurry and go around. Ronat's eyes darted to the thick under-brush, any place they might hide. Owen's hand gripped the hilt of his relative's blade, its weight foreign yet reassuring. Fiona had not had time to teach him much more than rudimentary swordplay.

"Left—now!" Ronat veered sharply. Owen obeyed instinctively, his heart pounding in his ears. A blur of movement—a guard lunged from the brush, steel glinting in the dawn light.

Ronat twisted, her cloak flaring, and a vine shot from the ground, ensnaring the guard's ankle. He fell with a grunt, his sword skittering away into the underbrush. They didn't stop.

"Another one!" Owen called out, as the silhouette of a second assailant took form ahead of them.

"Leave him to me," Ronat murmured, fingers dancing in the air, weaving another spell. A gust of wind howled, snatching leaves and debris, pelting the advancing guard. He shielded his face, stumbling backward.

"Quickly, this way." Ronat led them beneath a fallen tree, the bark moist and mossy against Owen's palm.

Arrows whistled, embedding in trees with soft thuds. Close. Too close. Owen felt a surge of panic, but he swallowed it down, meeting Ronat's gaze. Her determination buoyed him and quelled the tremor in his hands.

"Keep moving," she urged, her voice barely above a whisper.

As they moved through the slick terrain, the sounds of pursuit grew distant, then ominously silent. Owen's breath came in sharp gasps, clouding the chill air.

A sudden shout ripped through the quiet. Guards materialized on either side, closing in like wolves. Ronat stood back to back with Owen, her stance wide, ready.

"Fight as one," she breathed, and the forest itself seemed to lean in, listening.

Owen nodded, summoning all that Fiona had taught him, scant though it was. His grip on the blade steadied. Together, they faced the onslaught, brother and sister united.

Chapter 16

Captured

The iron beast roared, a sound of grinding gears and clashing metal that echoed through the once tranquil forest. Trees toppled and underbrush gave way to the relentless advance of Lady Abria's newest terror—a leviathan of steel and steam that consumed the earth beneath its treads. Owen, his hands bound, felt each shuddering step of the monstrosity as it carried him and Ronat up the steep incline of the ridge.

Ronat's eyes, usually alive with the whispering secrets of the woods, now reflected the smothered flames of her spirit. The machine disregarded nature's plea, indifferent to the destruction it wrought, much like the cold hearts of those who had invented it.

Although they had fought with courage, the siblings' stand against the Arran guards was brief. Their weapons stripped from them, hands bound, they were marched to this ghastly machine with its spiked caterpillar tracks and broad, iron clearing blade. Shoved in through a hatch in the roof, they were helpless passengers, unwilling witnesses to the tank's wanton destruction.

At the summit, the gondola tower pierced the sky, a barb of stone perched atop the world. It was here Lady Abria awaited, draped in a gown of crimson silk with a high, stiff collar of black lace, much different from the more modest clothing Owen was accustomed to seeing her in. Her guards pulled Owen and Ronat from the belly of the steam-belching beast.

"Welcome, my dearest niece and nephew," Lady Abria's voice crackled and hissed around them, charged with malice. She clapped her hands and her guards ushered Owen and Ronat toward the lobby of the tower. In the shafts of sunlight and shadow, stood too small cages, each just large enough for one prisoner.

Owen's gaze fell upon the bars, dark and dense. Magnetite. Known to disrupt the subtle energies of Fae magic, the mineral exuded an oppressive aura. He could see Ronat's muscles tense, the instinctual urge to rebel against the unnatural confines. Did she know what the material was? She held silent, her jaw set.

The guards shackled their wrists and ankles with cold efficiency before thrusting them into their respective prisons. Confinement—a concept so alien to Ronat, who had danced with the winds and conversed with the streams—was now her reality. Owen found himself cursing the ingenuity of Arran with even more intensity than usual.

Lady Abria circled the cages, her eyes gleaming with triumph. "These will hold you well enough," she gloated. "Your little tricks won't save you here."

Ronat met the woman's gaze; she was her aunt by blood, but no kinswoman to her. The girl spat onto the polished stone of the lobby floor, her spittle landing on one of Lady Abria's red velvet shoes. She made a face before pointing to her foot. A lackey emerged, wiping the damp stain with efficiency before Abria lifted the foot and gave him a kick, sending him sprawling and scuttling back into the shadows.

The echo of Lady Abria's laughter chilled the air in the tower. She twirled a small, now dull stone between her fingers, the touchstone Owen had carried for days. A beacon masquerading as protection.

"Did you really think this was to guide you?" she sneered, eyes alight with malice. "It guided *me*, dear nephew. To you ... and ultimately to your mother."

Owen's pulse quickened, confusion and dread knotting his stomach. "What do you mean?"

"Your precious mother, Queen Deirdre," Lady Abria spat the title like it was a bitter taste on her tongue. "She does live. For now. I've known since the beginning. And thanks to this," she held up the touchstone, "I'll find her at the bottom of the gorge and end her pitiful existence."

Desperation clawed at Owen; he must reach his mother, warn her!

"Father ..." His voice cracked, a feeble attempt to summon help from the man who should have been his protector. "Where is he?"

69

Lady Abria's smile twisted into something grotesque. She pointed upward, toward the sky, and for a moment, Owen thought of heaven. But then his eyes followed her gesture, up, higher still, to the observation deck of the gondola tower. There, King Athos stood, a silhouette against the sky, distant and unmoving.

"Father!" Owen's call tore from his lungs, raw and edged with betrayal. He saw the figure above pause, just for an instant, and then turn away, dismissing his son's plea without a backward glance.

Realization struck Owen with the force of a physical blow. His father, the king, complicit in this wickedness. Abandoned by blood, he was left to watch helplessly as his mother faced her doom.

"Now, you see ..." Lady Abria gave her nephew one last look, sending a contemptuous gaze toward the wild-looking Ronat before turning on her heel and leaving her captives under the watch of the guards. "I shall return when the deed is done. Then decisions will be made."

Owen watched his aunt leave. Through the door of the tower he saw Sir Galvrey meet her and lead Lady Abria toward the horrible machine. There were sounds of bellows being worked, coal blazing, and water gurgling as it became steam. The gearwheels of the tank whirred, and it shuddered to life once more, to begin its slow but relentless descent to the bottom of the gorge.

Owen's fists clenched as he sat with knees drawn to his chest; the cage was too low for pacing. Ronat watched him. Her eyes reflected back to him the defiance he felt within.

"Owen," she whispered. "We can't give up. There must be a way out."

He halted mid-stride, turned to her, his eyes misting over. "Oh, Ronat. This is all my fault. I dragged you into this."

"How?" She looked at him, puzzled. The question was not rhetorical.

"If you'd never met me, you never would have joined our quest. You'd be happy now, living your forest life, instead of caged like a ferocious beast."

"Why would anyone cage a ferocious beast?"

70

Owen couldn't help but laugh as he realized how different his world was from Ronat's.

She ran her knuckles against the bars, making the magnetite ring out. "I know they think these bars will hold us, dampen my power, but there's one thing I might try."

"Tell me!"

"A Narra cry. A call to summon my parents, Nochtan and Boann. If they hear me, they will come."

"Will it work?"

"It has to. The cry is not bound by Fae magic alone—it's a sound, a frequency that only Narra Fae can hear. The magnetite may not block it completely."

"Then do it." Owen's nod was a command, a plea, a vow all at once, beseeching her. "Call them."

Ronat pressed her forehead against the cool metal, closing her eyes. She inhaled deeply, gathering every ounce of her will.

"Be ready," she said, voice barely a whisper, as one of Lady Abria's guards peered from his post at the entrance, suspicion raised by the snatches of conversation. "When they come, we move quickly."

Inhale. Exhale. Focus. Ronat's lips parted, and from deep within her chest rose a sound, pure and piercing, the secret tone of the Narra Fae—a cry for help that soared beyond the confines of the cage, carrying all their hopes with it. Owen strained his ears, catching fractured pieces of the sound.

"Can you hear it?" Her voice was strained with effort, but her expression was hopeful.

"No," Owen admitted, frustration knitting his brow. His expression shifted. "Wait! Yes! In parts. It's there, then it isn't."

The sound continued, even more deeply felt now. Ronat's face twisted in concentration, her body a conduit for the ancient call.

But the air shivered, tinged with a discordant echo. The note wavered, recoiling off the magnetite like ripples against a jagged shore. It boxed them in, an invisible barrier smothering the call within the confines of their prison.

"Something's wrong." Panic edged into Ronat's voice.

Owen watched helplessly as the note turned on itself, a cruel inversion of intent. The cry that should have flown free now battered Ronat, sending her flying against the walls of the cage.

"Stop!" The command tore from him, more plea than order. "It's not working."

Ronat sagged against the bars, the sound dying on her lips.

Owen moved as close as he could to Ronat's cage. His voice was steady as he spoke. "Teach me."

"Owen, it—" Ronat hesitated, her gaze uncertain.

"Please." He wasn't above begging. Not now. Not with their mother's life hanging by a thread, not with Lyr missing and their own fates locked away in these cages.

"Alright." She straightened up, determination hardening her features once more. "Listen closely."

He nodded, pressing his forehead against the cool magnetite.

"Shape your breath," she instructed. "Let it coil within you. Build it up from the silence."

Owen closed his eyes, focusing on the rhythm of his breathing. In and out. A silent crescendo building inside him.

"Now, let it out—gently at first, then with all the force of the gale winds."

His lips parted, the breath slipping through them in a hesitant whistle. He adjusted, tried again, stronger this time. The sound was small and fragile, a tentative thread reaching for the unseen.

"Good," Ronat encouraged. "Now, imagine it piercing through stone and iron, beyond these bars."

Owen pictured the forests of Narra, the freedom and magic that he imagined thrived there. He anchored his desire in the call, a plea to the wind, to the earth, to water and fire. His whistle grew sharper, louder, a clear tone slicing through the heavy, stagnant air of the tower.

But then it happened.

The chilling vibration struck back, rebounding off the bars with a vengeance. It hammered into Owen, an invisible force that rattled his bones and shook his soul. His knees buckled, but he caught himself.

"Owen!" Ronat reached out, her arms dangling helplessly in the space between the two cages. "It can't be ..."

He met her gaze, the truth laid bare between them. The same echo that had rebuffed Ronat now worked against him, its resonance too familiar, too personal. It spoke of lineage, of blood ties to the mystical, of a heritage he'd never contemplated.

"Ronat ..." Owen began, unable to control the quiver in his voice. "I'm like you. I must be."

Chapter 17

Bixby of Arran

Understanding dawned in her eyes, a mixture of awe and sorrow. "You're part Fae, brother. The bars ... they wouldn't stop you if you weren't."

The implications were staggering, both terrifying and wondrous. Owen felt the ground beneath him shift, not in truth, but in everything he thought he knew. Magic surged within him, a dormant power awakened by the very trial meant to suppress it.

"Are you saying," Owen began, the implications dawning on him, "that we're both part Narra?"

"Both of us," Ronat confirmed, her voice tinged with excitement and sorrow. "It explains so much, doesn't it? Your love for magic, my life in the woods ... We are children of two worlds."

Owen's eyes met hers. They were kin not just by blood, but by spirit, bound by an ancient lineage. His mind sped through the memories of a childhood where he always felt at odds with the world he was born into. "How can it be?"

"Magic has its ways," Ronat replied, her voice soft but assured. "And sometimes, fate waits for the right moment to tip its hand."

"Under such dark clouds," Owen mused, tears pooling in his eyes. "I wish I had known sooner. I wish I had always known."

Ronat sighed. "Me too."

Her sigh turned into a gasp as the clank of steel against stone invaded the tower. She and Owen looked up to see King Athos descending the spiraling stairs of the gondola tower. The cold air seemed to follow him, a silent procession that chilled the room. He approached the cage where Owen, his face etched with confusion and hurt, stared up at him through iron bars.

But Athos offered no sign of recognition. No warmth touched his eyes; they were like chips of flint, sparking only with self-interested purpose.

Seized by rage, Owen cried out, "I am Owen! Your one and only son! Your heir!" The word sounded strange to him, all of a sudden. What was an heir? How could you inherit what you did not want? What only circumstance held you to?

But Athos' gaze did not waver; his face seemed to be made of the same stone as the tower. "Lady Abria's intent to end you will be thwarted," he decreed, voice devoid of paternal care if not kingly responsibility. "But your fate remains to be sealed away from the world."

"Imprisoned?" Owen's disbelief rang clear. "Forever?"

"Such is the necessity," Athos replied, turning his back on them both, as if concluding an insignificant transaction. Not once had he acknowledged Ronat's presence. If he realized who she was, he made no sign of it.

"Father, how can you be so cruel?" Owen cried out.

King Athos paused, shoulders rigid under his cloak. He faced his son, delivering his justification like a final verdict. "Cruelty is a matter of perspective, Owen. Commerce, technology—these are the sinews and bones of Arran. They forge empires, sustain populations, create manly order from natural chaos."

"Yet what of family? Of feeling?"

"Sentiment is the folly of the weak. It blinds rulers to the harsh truths of dominion. Only through discipline and the unyielding pursuit of progress can a kingdom stand mighty. *My* lineage has always understood this. And as for family ..."

Now, for the first time, he looked directly at Ronat. His gaze was charged with contempt. He knew her, but she had been dead to him for a long time. "The bonds of family are not nearly so sacred as is so often said."

With those words hanging in the air, King Athos turned and started to walk toward the tower doors.

The air crackled. A flash of brilliant light erupted, casting elongated shadows across the cold stone floor. Owen squinted against the sudden brightness, a sharp snap assaulting his ears followed by a billowing puff of smoke that unfurled like a flag in the wind.

As the smoke dissipated, a bewildering sight confronted them. Owen and Ronat stood in the middle of the polished floor while King Athos sat trapped within the very cage his son had occupied moments ago. His eyes, wide with disbelief, swept across his new, limited domain, his hands grasping at the iron bars that mocked his authority.

"Freedom," Ronat breathed out. She stepped forward, feeling the open space around her. Owen stood in a daze, still processing the reversal of their fates.

Laughter, light and mischievous, echoed through the chamber. From the corners and hidden niches emerged Nochtann and Boann, their forms dancing like the shimmer of sunlight on water. They spun and bounced around each other, their mirth a stark contrast to the severity of the scene they had altered.

"Playful as ever," Ronat muttered with an affectionate roll of her eyes.

Lyr emerged from the shadows. Her thoughts brushed against Owen's mind, a comforting whisper without words. He knew then, without doubt, she was the silent conductor of this orchestrated chaos—the summoner of the Narra Fae.

"King Athos," Owen said, duplicating Lyr's telepathic voice, "your reign of cages ends."

The king spat a curse, his face reddening with rage and humiliation. But no decree or command could free him from his prison.

Ronat looked at Nochtan and Boann, still playing hide-and-seek in the recesses of the tower. "Enough games," she said sternly, though her voice held an undercurrent of warmth. She gestured towards Owen, who stood wide-eyed beside her. "This is Owen, my brother."

"Ah, young prince," Boann's voice was a serene melody, "we've known you since you were but a whisper in the wind."

"Yes, just a wee fart!" Nochtan boomed, doubling over with laughter. Ronat looked at him disapprovingly.

"Known me?" Owen's brow creased with confusion.

"Let us share a tale." Nochtan's form shimmered as he spoke, his tone now mock-serious. "The story of Bixby of Arran and a love that birthed a curse."

"Your ancestor," Boann continued, her voice harmonizing with Nochtan's narrative, "while surveying the river, ventured deep into our valleys. There his heart was captured by a Fae maiden's charm."

"Yet," Nochtan's face darkened, "his love was a guise for greed. He trapped her within iron walls, twisted her magic to feed his hunger for power."

"Her sorrow," Boann whispered, "fueled his machines, tore the land asunder."

"But!" Nochtan interjected, "before this, the villain had struck a deal. To wed our kin, to let him claim her, a vow was made. Every fifth generation, a child to be raised by Fae."

"King Athos," Boann's lips curled into a sly smile, "was robbed of his wedding night, intoxicated on rivergrape wine. Who Queen Deirdre believed to be her new husband, was none other than Nochtan."

"What!" roared the humiliated king from his cage. His eyes bulged from their sockets, spittle gathering at the corners of his livid mouth.

"Yes. An illusion," Nochtan bowed mockingly, "to seal the pact with Fae magic."

"Thus," Boann concluded, her eyes meeting Ronat's, "you are nearly pure Narra, daughter of the forest and streams."

Ronat felt her world tilt once more. "Almost fully Narra," she repeated softly.

"And me?" Owen asked.

"Three tenths and one quarter," said Nochtan. "Your mother is part Narra as well. This thing," he continued, pointing a long toe at the caged king, "is nearly all mortal."

"I am!" Athos cried. "All mortal! 100% Arran. Not a drop of your contamination lives in my veins."

"Hm." Nochtan cocked his head. "Believe what you like."

The ground trembled beneath their feet, a low rumble escalating into a thunderous roar. It sounded as though Abria's mechanical monstrosity had just sheared one of the rocky outcrops of its ancient stone in its relentless descent to the bottom of Narra Gorge.

"Too late!" King Athos' voice sliced through the receding din. "My technology will reshape this world, regardless of blood or bond."

Chapter 18

The Cogsmen

Fiona's muscles tensed, her eyes locked on the massive boulder thundering down the slope like a wrathful god. Beside her, Cathal's breath caught, his diminutive form a contrast to her towering presence. "Jump!" she barked, and they hurled themselves aside, the ground shuddering as the boulder rolled past, missing them by mere inches.

The hillside groaned, spewing a churning river of dirt and stone in the wake of Abria's explosives. Fiona scrambled to her feet, a hand automatically reaching for the hilt of her sword, though it was no weapon against this onslaught. She searched desperately for Ronat and Owen, their figures swallowed by the billowing dust. "Ronat! Owen!" Her voice was lost in the noise of the landslide.

Cathal seized her arm, urgency in his face. "This way!" he shouted, gesturing towards a hollow beneath a rocky outcrop. They ducked and weaved, dodging flying debris with practiced agility. Cathal's training shone through even in flight, each movement precise and calculated. Next to him, Fiona found herself clumsy.

They reached the hollow. Cathal threw himself into its open mouth with Fiona at his heels. The guide fell on top of him. Rocks clattered around them as they lay in their accidental embrace, the world a maelstrom of noise and fury just beyond their sanctuary.

"Safe ... for now," Cathal panted. Fiona nodded, chest heaving. Silence stretched between them, punctuated by distant rumbles as they waited for the earth's rage to subside. Moments passed before they realized that they were still holding one another. They did not break the embrace. Cathal watched Fiona's eyes, his own open and honest, not hiding the feelings within. To his surprise, the guide took his chin in her rough hands and kissed him.

"There," she said. "Are you happy?"

But Cathal just sat there, stunned, a half-smile on his face.

Dust settled. Fiona stood; her keen eyes had caught on an anomaly—a door, half-concealed behind fallen rock. "Cathal," she said, her voice a hoarse whisper. "Look."

The ex-guard followed her line of sight, nodding. Together, they approached, muscles tensed for any sign of danger. The door was sturdy, metal-bound, incongruous with the natural hollow. Cathal's hand found a cold handle and turned it. A creak echoed as it gave way to darkness beyond.

"Looks like a maintenance corridor," Cathal observed, peering into the void.

"Must lead somewhere," Fiona agreed, stepping through the threshold. They used a hefty stone to prop the reluctant door open, unsure if it was a lucky break or a trap.

Eyes adjusting to the gloom, they trod the corridor, their footfalls swallowed by the earthen walls of the passageway. It stretched, turning and sloping gently downward. The last of the tremors faded into silence around them.

Some two hundred yards down, the corridor ended abruptly. A pile of rubble blocked further progress. Fiona's hands worked alongside Cathal's, grappling with stones, setting them aside with grunts of exertion.

At last, a dim light broke through. An opening, wide enough to step through.

"Hello?" Fiona called, her voice carrying.

Faces turned towards them—a group of a dozen Cogsmen, eyes wide with disbelief. The massive cogs in the gear room were still, the machinery at rest, the air thick with distrust and ... something else. Fiona found it in the faces of the men: resignation.

"Who are you?" one Cogsman asked, wary but hopeful.

"Friends," Fiona replied, her stature commanding attention despite the dirt smudging her features. "We're here to help."

A murmur rippled through the gathered laborers, relief mingling with confusion as they took in their unexpected rescuers.

Cathal stared at the dirty, exhausted Cogsmen and the gears. They were clearly not the series of automated pulleys and sluices he had imagined fueled the gondolas.

"Hydro-powered," Fiona muttered. "That's what we were told."

"Changed after the accident," a Cogsman spoke up, his voice hoarse. "They never fixed the hydro turbines. Since then, it's been us, turning these gears night and day."

"The poor king and queen ..." another laborer interjected, his eyes downcast. "We've been stuck down here since that day. And now we're trapped. Or were. Earth shook like the end of days. You must have felt it. Then, Abria's orders—stay put."

"Orders?" Cathal frowned. "How do you communicate?"

"Code. On the cables," explained a younger Cogsman. He walked toward a giant cable looped around the base of the gearwheel. They listened as he made a series of taps that resounded in the cavernous room.

"What was that?" asked Fiona.

"I just said, 'Welcome'."

Cathal scratched his chin. "I recognize that code."

"Ancient code. Gerr code. You know it?"

"Yes. My grandfather was a wheelwright. A member of your guild. He taught it to me."

Fiona broke in, impatiently. "But how do you leave and come back?"

"Door's one way," the younger Cogsman said, pointing in the direction they had come. "Only opens from the outside. Other way is up. But the ladder ... " He pointed upward to a ladder dangling several hundred feet above. "It was destroyed in the quake."

A cold realization washed over Fiona and Cathal. Lady Abria's treachery ran deeper than they knew. She had left these men to die, buried alive in their servitude. Fiona clenched her sword hilt tighter.

"Abria has gone too far," she declared, her voice cutting through the despair. The Cogsmen nodded, sadly. Some had looks of anger blossoming on their faces.

"Join us." Cathal stepped forward. "Against Abria. For freedom."

"A revolt?" A murmur spread, a spark of hope igniting in the Cogsmen's chests.

"A revolt," Fiona affirmed. "Lady Abria thinks you're dead. We'll show her otherwise."

Nods multiplied through the crowd. Whispers grew to words, words to chants as the Cogsmen rallied behind the call for justice.

"Revolt!" The word was a battle cry, reverberating off the stone walls.

"Revolt!" They echoed, each voice louder than the last.

"Revolt!" Fiona and Cathal led the charge, the Cogsmen at their backs as they began to tear the stones that still blocked much of the exit.

The passageway loomed dark and narrow ahead of Fiona. Cathal's hand found hers, a silent pact between them. Behind, the Cogsmen moved as one, a shadow serpent winding through the core of the hill.

Rocks grated beneath their boots, their breaths ragged. The claustrophobic walls seemed to pulse with anticipation. Every step was a march towards uncertainty, yet they pressed on, driven by the promise of retribution.

Daylight broke faintly ahead. They emerged one by one, squinting against the brightness. Fiona surveyed the ridge—it rose steep, a jagged staircase to the heavens. She hoisted herself up first, muscles protesting but her will ironclad. Cathal followed, nimble as a mountain goat, the mutineers clambering behind.

The gondola tower loomed, its guards unsuspecting. Fiona had no sympathy for these pawns in Abria's cruel game. The rebels fanned out, a wave about to crash. Fiona's sword gleamed. With a nod to Cathal, the signal was given.

"Charge!" she roared, her voice like thunder.

Chapter 19

Song of Stone

As one, they surged forward. The guards scrambled, weapons drawn too late. Steel clashed, and cries ripped through the air.

The skirmish was over swiftly, the element of surprise their greatest ally, evading the need to draw much blood. The guards lay subdued, shock on their faces. Fiona's gaze swept the base of the tower, searching for what they had come to find.

"Here," Cathal called, his voice an odd mixture of triumph and disbelief.

They entered the tower. There in the central hall were Ronat and Owen, Lyr perched on his shoulder. Inside one of two cages sat King Athos. His eyes blinked up at them. Surprise flared as he caught sight of the Cogsmen outside.

Owen ran to Fiona and hugged her. "We thought it was Abria's machine!"

"What machine?"

Owen's words tumbled out, a frantic cascade that tripped over Ronat's equally hurried explanations. "And Nochtan and Boann—they just appeared," he gasped, eyes wide with the shock of recent events.

"Summoned by Lyr!" Ronat interjected, as she gestured wildly toward the serpine, whose glossy coat bristled with pride.

"My father, he—" Owen started again, only to be cut off by his sister.

"Alive!"

"Yes," said Fiona, puzzledly. "I can see that."

"But where are your fae parents?" Owen spun around, searching the shadows for Nochtan and Boann. Ronat smiled, knowing their habits.

Cathal's hand went up, slicing through the air like a blade parting reeds. "Enough," he said, gently but with authority. Muscles still tense, Fiona nodded.

"My dear pups," Fiona began. "We'll sort it out later."

Dear pups? Lyr's purr struck a tone of irony. Owen could have giggled. But the word "pup" was Queen Deirdre's preferred term of endearment for him.

"We need to get to the gorge," he blurted out, his voice cutting through the lingering murmurs of confusion. "Abria is on her way there," he added, his gaze locked with Ronat's. He saw the realization dawn in her eyes, the awareness that their time was running short.

Fiona and Cathal exchanged looks. If this metal titan of Abria's was as powerful as Owen said it was, what hope did they have of reaching the queen before her?

"Can you—" Owen hesitated only for a fraction of a second, "—can you talk to the stones, again? Shape them into a path? Straight down to the gorge?"

Ronat's eyes sparkled with the challenge, the untamed part of her that thrived on the impossible stirring to life. "A rock-slide spell," she mused aloud, her fingers twitching as if already weaving the magic.

"Directly to the bottom?" Owen persisted, hope threading through his desperation.

"Never tried," she admitted, her mouth screwing up with concentration. "But with you ..." She trailed off, her implication hanging between them, almost a promise.

"Let's do it."

Owen's breaths came in sharp bursts as they left the gondola tower. The dirt-streaked Cogsmen stood at attention, forming a perimeter around the subdued guards. Owen thanked them without stopping, each man bowing as the prince passed.

Ronat led the way to the edge of the ridge where the steep descent began. Her steps were sure and swift. Coming up beside her, Fiona scanned the awesome depths of the gorge. Despite everything she had seen, the promises of magic still seemed too good to be true. Cathal discreetly pressed her hand, whispering in her ear to trust Ronat and Owen.

Quickly, Lyr urged, sniffing the breeze and glancing back at Owen. Her thoughts carried the urgency of a ticking clock.

They reached an open space where the hillside lay scattered with rocks. Here, Ronat turned to him, her expression serious. "After me," she instructed.

"O stones of old, hear my wish," she began, her words vibrating with power.

"O stones of old, hear my wish," Owen repeated, feeling the vibrations tickle his throat, foreign and yet familiar, like a language of childhood long unused.

"Bind together, bend to will," Ronat continued, her hands moving through the air as if conducting an invisible orchestra.

"Bind together, bend to will …"

"Form the path that we desire," Ronat's voice rose, a crescendo that matched the pulsing energy of the hillside.

"Form the path that we desire …"

"Guide our passage, swift and true," Ronat concluded, her eyes alight.

"Guide our passage, swift and true!"

The ground trembled beneath them, a deep rumble that grew in intensity until it was a roar. Rocks stirred, clinking against one another like the pieces of a giant puzzle finding their places. Larger stones rolled into position, while smaller pebbles and gravel filled the gaps. Before their eyes, the chaotic heap transformed, coalescing into a smooth, sloping structure that spiraled down towards the bottom of the gorge.

"By the Great Gears," Fiona breathed out, her usual stoicism giving way to awe.

Cathal let out a low whistle, his eyes wide with admiration for the spectacle before them.

Good, Owen. Lyr's tail tapped with excitement against Owen's ear. He stood amidst the magic he had helped weave, no longer the failed engineering student but a prince who had finally grasped his true calling. Together with Ronat, he had spoken to the very bones of the earth, and they had listened. They had obeyed.

Muscles strained and earth crunched underfoot. The old gondola, a relic of forgotten travels, resisted at first, its joints creaking in protest. Fiona's formidable strength set the pace, her arms flexing as she tugged on the rusted metal frame. Cathal, along with two Cogsmen, pushed from behind, grunting with the effort.

"Come on, heave ho!"

Owen's palms pressed against the cool surface, adding his meager physical might to the collective push. Beside him, Ronat's slender fingers traced symbols into the gondola's side, lending assurance to their mission.

"Steady!" Cathal warned as the gondola lurched forward with a groan, finally yielding to their efforts.

The contraption edged towards the rocky slide, metal scraping against stone. It was an awkward dance of old meeting new—ancient magic breathing life into the forgotten framework of a bygone era.

"Everyone in," Owen ordered, his voice shaky but carrying the weight of command.

One by one, they clambered into the weather-beaten vessel. Fiona hoisted herself up with ease and Cathal followed, nimble and quick.

Owen, came Lyr's voice. *I shall stay here.*

The prince turned to the serpine, a puzzled look on his face. "Why, Lyr?"

You will want someone here with whom you can communicate.

"Yes, I suppose that's right ..." Owen hesitated. He had only just gotten Lyr back. How was he supposed to leave her again?

It will be alright. Lyr coiled herself around Owen's leg, comforting him before streaking back toward the tower. Owen breathed in deeply. She was right, but it didn't make leaving her less difficult.

"Ready?" Ronat's eyes met Owen's.

"Ready."

With a collective heave, they pushed off.

Chapter 20

A Queen's Rescue

Gravity took hold, and the gondola hurtled down the magic slide. The wind in that high place howled, a banshee's cry that joined the screech of the metal gondola against the rocks. Downward they plunged, sparks flying, the gorge rising up to meet them, each twist and turn of the slide tossing them to one side and then the other.

Owen clutched the sides of the gondola, his face white with fear. But Ronat seemed to be enjoying herself, positioned at the front of the gondola, the wind whipping her long tresses behind her. Leaves and dust spiraled up from the woods below, caught in the backdraft of their breakneck speed.

"Brace yourself!" she shouted over the roar.

Owen dared a glance at Fiona, her muscular frame tense and alert, gripping the seat with one hand while securing Cathal with the other.

Below, the valley rushed up to meet them, and within it loomed Abria's monstrous creation. Owen could pinpoint the location of the abomination of engineering as it chewed through the landscape by the trees that fell all around it. He knew his aunt's cruelty well and now saw it manifest in iron and steam, ravaging the land he loved.

"Look out!" Cathal's shout snapped Owen back to reality just as their gondola took a sudden dip, stomachs lifting into throats. They were a box of rattling matchsticks flung from a giant's hand.

But then, as the ground rushed up with fatal certainty, the gondola jolted to an abrupt and improbable halt. The force whipped their heads forward, and for a moment, everything was still, save for the clatter of loose pebbles cascading down the slide behind them. Their breaths came in ragged gasps, incredulous at their own survival.

Owen's legs trembled as he stepped from the gondola onto solid ground. The others followed, their movements hesitant, disoriented by the sudden stillness, avoiding the metal frame of the gondola, piping hot from the friction of their harrowing descent. He spared a glance upwards where the slide had soared moments before. Now, there was only empty air.

Spellbound, Owen witnessed the magic unraveling. Each stone lifted, hovered, and drifted back to its place with an ethereal grace. The landscape mended itself seamlessly, as if the earth remembered where every rock belonged. The slide that had borne them so recklessly down the gorge ceased to exist, leaving no scar upon the land.

"Come on," Fiona urged.

With the spell broken, they sought a path forward. The giant gondola cable, thick as a man's waist, snaked through the gorge beside a shallow river. It led them onward, the water murmuring over rocks like a secret conversation.

They had been walking for several hours, the sun already disappearing over the ridge, when a cottage appeared on the other side of the river. Thatched roof, walls of wattle and daub, it spoke of a life far removed from Arran's opulence. Outside, between two young but sturdy willow trees, a hammock was strung. A figure wrapped in blankets, head swathed in white bandages, lay inside.

"Mother?" Owen's voice faltered as he ran, tripping over the stones of the river, which at its deepest point reached only above his knees. He threw himself on the patch of grass by the hammock and knelt beside it.

Queen Deirdre lay motionless inside. Her chest rose and fell with such faintness, she seemed barely tethered to life. Owen's heart clenched at the sight of her pallor, her stillness evoking images of eternal slumber.

"Your majesty?" Cathal called softly, climbing up the river bank with Fiona and Ronat behind him.

No response came from the hammock's fragile occupant. Shadows played across her closed eyelids, lashes casting delicate patterns upon her cheeks. Owen knew it would take more than gentle words to wake her from her deep repose. He stepped closer, his own breath held hostage by apprehension and hope.

His hand hovered over the queen's pale face. A touch could shatter her fragile peace—or call her back to them.

"Wait," a voice broke through his concentration. Two figures emerged from the cottage, their appearances rough-hewn and earthy. They moved with purpose, their hands worn by toil but their eyes alight with something unbroken. These were not mere peasants; they bore themselves with the quiet dignity of those who had seen much and chosen their path with care.

"Who goes there?" Fiona's hand was on her sword.

"Friends," said one, a woman with hair like autumn leaves. "We are—were—engineers for the House of Arran."

"Turned healers for the queen," the man beside her added. He was broad-shouldered, with hands that looked capable of wrestling a tree to the ground yet held a gentle calm as he approached Deirdre.

"Her injuries were grave," the woman continued. "We've done what we can with herbs, fresh water, and rest."

"Magic has helped," the man said, glancing curiously at Ronat.

"Magic? Of what kind?"

"Fae magic." The woman's smile was knowing. "We've been living off this land, in harmony with the Narra."

"Learning their ways," the man chimed in.

"A truce of sorts. Building bridges of a different sort," the woman finished.

Owen felt the tension ease from his shoulders. Here stood allies in a world that seemed increasingly set upon their ruin. Perhaps there was hope yet for both Arran and Fae. For his family.

"Thank you," he whispered, grateful for their guardianship over his mother. And for the first time since the gondola's wild descent, he allowed himself to believe in the possibility of healing—not just for the queen, but for the torn fabric of their world.

In her sling, Deirdre murmured. Owen could not contain himself much longer. He let his hand stroke her face. Her eyes fluttered.

"Owen ...?" The queen's eyes were barely open, but a weak smile brightened her face.

Turning to Ronat, Owen reached for her hand. "Mother," he began, voice trembling with emotion, "there is someone I want you to meet."

Now Deirdre's eyes opened fully, deep green, clear and piercing. The corners of her mouth lifted slightly, a softness there that belied the pain she must have felt.

"This is Ronat," Owen said, guiding Ronat closer. "Or Emyr. Your daughter. My sister."

Ronat knelt beside the hammock, her gaze locked with Deirdre's. There was a shimmer in the air, like before a storm. A mother's recognition bloomed silently but undeniably.

"Emyr," Deirdre breathed out, her voice laden with years of unspoken longing and love. She reached out, her pale hand shaking as it sought Ronat's.

Ronat took the offered hand, her own fingers closing around it with a careful tenderness. "Mother," she tried, the word strange and new.

The moment stretched, fragile and poignant. For those few heartbeats, nothing existed beyond the small clearing, the rustic cottage, and the silent reunion of a mother with her children.

But peace, like silence, is easily broken.

A distant rumble intruded upon the scene, growing louder, more insistent. It was the sound of inevitability, of approaching doom—the mechanical roar of Abria's machine tearing through the valley.

Ronat's head snapped up, her eyes narrowing. The grip on her mother's hand tightened protectively. Owen stood, every muscle taut, as the former engineers exchanged worried glances behind them.

"What's this?" Owen said, noticing a stone around the neck of the woman for the first time. His eyes bulged. The stone was identical to the touchstone, right down to the same, gentle pulsating glow.

"Your mother, the queen ..." began the woman."She was wearing it. I said I would keep it safe for her while she recovered."

"Mother?"

"Yes, dear boy?"

"Where did you get this?"

"It was a gift. Your father gave it to me, or perhaps it was your aunt. An anniversary present."

"No!" Owen could not control himself. He nearly tore the stone from the cottager's neck. She startled, unclasped the chain, and handed him the stone. Placing it on a river-stone, Owen smashed it with the butt of his sword.

But it was too late. There was a brief pause as their location had disappeared from Abria's radar. Still, the device had led her to them. She knew that they were just ahead, on the other side of the river.

The machine started up again and the sound thundered closer, almost upon them, a harbinger of destruction that threatened to tear apart what little hope they'd managed to find in this hidden refuge.

Chapter 21

The Forest Rises

Ancient twigs snapped like twigs, heralded the approach of Lady Abria's war engine.

"What is it?" asked the man, the former engineer.

"Something hideous," Owen answered. "Monstrous machines that tear senselessly through the heart of these woods, carrying Abria to her prize."

"What does she want?"

"Us." Owen clutched a gnarled root at the riverbank, his soul recoiling from each violent thud that vibrated through the earth and into his bones.

In the clear water of the river, seemingly oblivious to the destruction afoot, two golden fish swam around one another, circling and circling one another, as if in play.

There was a sudden surge of water beside Owen as the fish leapt into the air, their forms shimmering and stretching. In the blink of an eye, where once swam creatures of scale and fin now stood Nochtan and Boann.

As if summoned by their rulers' transformation, other Narra materialized from the forest and the rippling veil of the river—a legion of ethereal warriors, features chiseled from the shapes of tree and rock, eyes alight with ancient mirth. They encircled Ronat and Queen Deirdre, a silent vow of protection echoing in the stillness between each deafening crash of Abria's advance.

Boann raised her arms, palms skyward. Her lips moved in an incantation that stirred the leaves and set the very air alive with potential. The woods responded, tree limbs intertwining and stems coiling, an arboreal loom operated by the Fae queen.

"Look!" Ronat yelled, as Abria's tread machine reached the opposite bank of the river, bursting out of the forest.

All eyes turned toward the machine as thick vines erupted from the soil, coiling serpent-like around the mechanized monstrosities that dared invade their sanctum. Trees, ancient and indomitable, bent their boughs protectively, roots writhing from the ground to ensnare wheels and immobilize gears. The relentless march of Abria's tank faltered, its metallic frame groaning under nature's reclaiming grasp.

Owen watched, standing protectively by the queen, as Boann harnessed the latent power of the woods. Each vine and branch moved with purpose, guided by an unseen force.

Magic pulses strong in the valleys of Arran, he thought. *It will not yield its domain without a fight.*

Meanwhile, in the shadowed undergrowth, Nochtan's body contorted once more. With a flicker of magic, the King of the Narra Fae turned himself into a field mouse, whiskers twitching with anticipation. Around him, a number of other Narra followed suit, their bodies shrinking, fur sprouting, and eyes brightening with rodent resolve.

The newly transformed mice scurried toward the besieged machine, slipping through tiny gaps in the metal hull. Owen watched, holding his breath, as Nochtan and his contingent vanished into the bowels of Abria's mechanical beast.

Inside, the tiny saboteurs set to work. Teeth sharper than any artisan's tool gnawed at tubes and cables, severing the sinews of war. They burrowed into bellows, their incisors cutting swathes through the leather that controlled the flow of steam. The tank groaned, metal innards exposed to the wild assault, as vital connections were chewed apart and rendered useless.

Now the engines sputtered, steam hissing from its wounds. Soon, the machine ground to a complete halt, any struggle it may have made against its natural restraints frustrated by the smallest of foes.

The mice retreated from the machine, Nochtan and the others assuming their regular forms. Boann's hands dropped; the vines and tree boughs hardened in place, securing their quarry.

Lady Abria remained trapped within her flagship tank, her face a mask of seething rage visible through the narrow slit of her viewing port. She had banked on iron and steam to secure her victory, never expecting nature—or its diminutive guardians—to rise against her.

Owen approached the silent behemoth, his heart jumping against his ribs. "Aunt Abria," he called, his voice steady in spite of the turmoil within. "Surrender is your only option now."

Her response was silence, a cold void where words might have been. He pressed closer, peering into the darkened interior, catching glimpses of her steely glare.

"Talk to me," Owen urged, knowing the futility even as he spoke. "We can end this without further bloodshed."

But Abria would not dignify his plea with a response. Imprisoned in her creation, she seemed less a conqueror now and more a monument to her own obstinacy. Her lips pressed into a tight line, and her eyes burned with undiminished malice. There would be no parley, no concession—only the quiet fury of a tyrant thwarted by the very land she sought to subjugate.

Resigned, Owen stepped back, leaving her to stew in the tomb of her ambition. He turned to the others, his expression somber yet resolute. They understood the unspoken command: they would move forward, with or without Lady Abria's cooperation.

Their gaze swept over the wreckage strewn across the forest floor, remnants of a battle between the ancient magic of the land and the mechanical horror his aunt had unleashed. Ronat stayed with Deirdre as Fiona and Cathal joined Owen around the hulking mass of metal that trapped Lady Abria within.

Owen suddenly felt exhausted, wearier than his scant years should permit. "What should we do with it?"

"Let's bind it to the gondola cable," Fiona suggested. "We'll have the Cogsmen drag this beast back up the hillside, carve a trail of penitence through the destruction it sowed." Her muscular arms flexed as she considered the task, a physical challenge that seemed to invigorate her spirit.

"And what about my aunt?"

Cathal leaned toward the viewing portal. "Will you neither come out nor speak, Lady?" No answer. "We can't leave her in there like this, can we?" Owen asked.

Nochtan, with a glimmer of mischief in his eyes, stepped forward. His hands moved through the air, sketching symbols only the Fae understood, and they tittered amongst themselves knowing what was to come. Lady Abria's form glittered, and where the imperious woman once sat, there now perched a tiny brown sparrow, delicate and disoriented. Nochtan offered a nod to Fiona, who opened her satchel and allowed the bird to hop inside, safely nestled amidst the leather folds.

"Keep watch," he said to Fiona, a warning laced with a smile. "She's still dangerous, even with wings."

With the plan set, Owen closed his eyes and reached out with his mind, seeking the familiar presence of Lyr. He imagined the thread of their connection stretching out over the distance, trying to tug on the Cogsmen's awareness through the animal's keen senses. But the mental call waned, melting away before it could bridge the gulf that separated him from Lyr.

He opened his eyes, frustration on his face. "It's too far," he admitted, rubbing at his temples where the strain of effort lingered. "The message won't reach."

"Then we'll do it the old way," Cathal said, his optimism undimmed. His fingers traced the frayed end of the gondola cable. He tapped it lightly, a rhythmic thudding that resonated through the metal strands. The sound traveled along the cable, vibrations traveling up the hill.

"Remember, this can carry more than just people."

Owen turned to him, not understanding. Cathal struck the cable again, harder this time, the *tap-tap-tap* a staccato beat against the hush of the woods. "Gerr code."

Recognition dawned on Owen. Yes! For once he recalled one of his readings at the engineering academy. "Gerr code––the ancient tapping code of the Wrights."

"Correct," said Cathal. "Like a giant telegraph," he mused aloud. "If we can send taps through the lines, Lyr and the Cogsmen might hear us."

"Brilliant," Owen breathed, his impatience turning to hopeful anticipation.

Fiona crouched by the cable, her powerful hands feeling out its length. She gave an approving nod. "Signal them to wind it up on our mark."

Cathal bent over the cable, the teachings of his grandfather returning to him. He hesitated only momentarily before his fingers danced a precise pattern upon its surface. Each deliberate tap was a call to action, sent through the veins of Arran itself.

They waited, hearts thumping not from exertion but from the suspense of silent prayers. Moments stretched, until faintly, almost imperceptibly, a series of returning taps echoed back to them.

"Understood," Cathal translated with a relieved grin. "They're ready."

Chapter 22

Ascension

They set to work, fastening thick, coiled cables around the inert colossus. Each clank of metal echoed a promise to restore what had been torn asunder.

As they prepared to haul the machine up the mountain pass, Owen knew the journey would be grueling. But with every step, they carried not just the dead weight of iron and ambition but the hopes of a land yearning for healing.

With the communication line established, Owen and Fiona busied themselves with the next critical task. The one-time engineers gave them their very own pallet, which Fiona hoisted into Abria's machine, its structure firm enough to bear the weight of a queen yet soft enough to cushion her injuries.

"How does it look in there?" Owen called down to Fiona when she was inside the tank.

"I've never seen anything like it," replied the guide, utterly bewildered by so many buttons, knobs and levers.

"No! I mean the bed ..."

Fiona laughed. "Oh, I'm sorry, pup. It's all ready. Fit for a queen."

Owen groaned. Earlier, while they thought he wasn't looking, he had spotted Cathal stroking her hand. Was this what Fiona in love was going to be like?

Ronat lingered by the queen, her hands fluttering like moth wings. She was nervous. Her gaze lingered on Deirdre's pallid face, the magic within her stirring with a blend of concern and duty. She reached out, her touch gentle as if fearing the fragility of human form, despite it being her own.

"Be easy," she whispered, her voice carrying the lilt of the woods. The queen stirred under her ministrations, a faint sigh escaping her lips.

"Care for her, Ronat," Owen urged, his tone laced with familial worry. "She'll need all your skills."

"Of course, brother," Ronat replied, offering him a small, reassuring smile. "I've learned much from the Fae, but I haven't completely lost our human ways."

Together, they secured the queen, binding her gently to the pallet inside the machine.

"Ready?" Fiona asked, her voice steady as the bedrock beneath them.

"Ready."

"Then let's bring our queen home," Cathal added.

Fiona's arms, thick with sinew and scars, flexed as she checked the metal cable hitched to the gondola. "Secured," she grunted, satisfaction deep in her voice.

She and Cathal mounted the tank; they would ride uphill on its metal hull, while Ronat and Owen kept watch over the queen inside.

Before they left, Owen made sure to thank the man and woman whose names he had not even had time to learn. The woman, Belinda; the man, John.

"Please come to the castle, once everything settles down," Owen urged them. "I would like to thank you properly. With food and wine and, and ..."

"Knowing that we could be of service to the good and gentle queen is thanks enough," Belinda softly interrupted him. Although they were still half-strangers, she put her arms around the prince and hugged him tight.

Far, far above, unheard by the questers, the winch of the gondola tower groaned into life, gears biting into the cable as the Cogsmen began their arduous task. Below, in the gorge, the river receded slowly, the heavy machinery beginning its painstaking climb.

The Narra couple accompanied them on foot. Around them, Boann's magic whispered through the trees; branches unfurled, leaves stitched together the torn earth, and flowers bloomed where destruction once reigned. The land healed, a tapestry of greenery weaving over the scars of demolition.

As they ascended, Owen and Ronat stood vigilant around the bed where the queen lay, each lost in their own thoughts as they left the gorge floor behind.

They remained like this for what felt like an eternity––watchful and thoughtful, wincing with each bump that jostled the queen in her bed. Upon cresting the ridge, the treetops seemed to bow below, the newly regrown forest a sea of tranquility after the tumultuous journey. The gondola tower loomed ahead, its structure stark against the twilit sky.

They came to rest at the foot of the tower with an abrupt halt that jostled the passengers. Queen Deirdre groaned.

As they unloaded the precious cargo, Nochtan, ethereal as always, approached King Athos, still restrained and silent within his metallic prison. The Fae king's eyes glinted once more with mischief and, in a shimmer of light, King Athos' form shrank and twisted, reshaping into the delicate body of a sparrow equal to that of Abria's, feathers the color of dried twigs. He flapped around in confusion before settling, a captive of his new form.

"Here, you go with your sister," Fiona said, her voice betraying a hint of amusement as she carefully deposited the sparrow king into her satchel. It bulged slightly, containing the winged monarch alongside his sister.

"Let's not have any pecking in there," she warned the bag, before slinging it over her shoulder with a grunt.

The party exchanged glances, weary but resolute, shared purpose shining in their eyes. They were ready to face the next leg of their journey, but looking down at the slack cable as it ran through two valleys before rising to the final gondola quay of Arrantown, their hearts sank.

How could they possibly carry the injured queen that distance?

Chapter 23

Homecoming

With deft hands and eager murmurs, the Cogsmen swarmed the gondola tower, shining in the early morning light. They had been working since first light. The sounds of their repairs woke the others in their makeshift camp on the main floor of the tower. Metal clanked against metal, gears turned in harmony, and with each tightened bolt and secured cable, their spirits lifted as they prepared themselves for the day.

The Cogsmen had witnessed Queen Deirdre's fall, her plunge into the abyss of treachery designed by those of her own blood. Witnessed not by seeing but by feeling. While they ensured the proper workings of the gearworks, they had felt the cable go suddenly slack when the royal gondola was midway between towers. Yet here she was, battered but breathing—their beacon of hope in a kingdom too long riddled with shadows.

"Nearly there!" shouted one of the Cogsmen, his voice echoing off the steel beams as he gave the newly-affixed cable a last tug. The taut structure seemed to hum with readiness, prepared to cradle its precious cargo back to Arrantown.

Owen, the first to rise, stretching his stiff muscles, stood nearby, his youthful face drawn with concern as he watched his mother lying still on the makeshift stretcher. The subtlety of the rise and fall of her chest left a tightness in his own. He felt Ronat's hand on his shoulder.

"Will it hold?" Owen asked, looking up to where the cable was being mended.

"Trust in their craft. Their joy in seeing the queen safe will not allow for failure."

Fiona nodded in agreement. "Come, Cathal, Lyr. It's almost ready."

Lyr climbed up to the prince's shoulder, rubbing her muzzle against his cheek, offering calm and wordless reassurance. The serpine could sense the nervous energy emanating from his body.

At last, the Cogsmen descended. The foreman stepped back. He offered a grimy hand to Owen. "She will reach Arrantown safely, my Prince."

With a collective breath, the group moved, lifting the stretcher bearing the queen to the platform and onto the waiting gondola. The cabin swayed slightly as it accepted the weight, the cables above groaning their steadfast and familiar song. As the doors closed, sealing them within, Owen took his place beside his mother, his hand finding hers.

"Let's go home," he whispered.

The gondola lurched forward, embarking on its journey across the two chasms that separated them from the city. Below, the world stretched out in waves of verdant forests and jagged cliffs—a land that had nearly claimed them all.

Ronat leaned close to the glass, her eyes reflecting the wild beauty outside. She couldn't help but admire the ingenuity of the gondola.

"Look," Fiona said softly, gesturing toward the horizon where Arrantown's spires jutted into the sky like silver needles.

Cathal watched the approaching city, his thoughts unreadable. But when Fiona reached for his hand, he didn't hesitate, their fingers entwining—a silent pact forged in the heat of battle.

The gondola lurched, a groan of twisted metal riding the chill breeze. Owen's heart skipped, his fingers tightening around the queen's hand. Ronat's eyes shot upwards, trying to track the sound to its source. Another mishap?

The gondola steadied, resuming its dance with gravity as Arrantown drew closer, the city's gates opening like an embrace.

"Almost there," Owen murmured, his eyes locked onto his mother's peaceful face.

At the quay, the guards assembled, a line of solemn faces and polished armor. Their eyes lit upon the queen's form, cradled in the arms of her children, and respect softened their features. They stepped forward, hands outstretched, ready to bear Deirdre home.

Owen recoiled. "No!" How could he trust these guards after what Abria had done to them?

Cathal stepped forward, his head lowered as he spoke to the captain of the guards. "This man can be trusted," he said to Owen. "I would stake my life on it, for I have known him all of mine."

"Thank you," Owen said, his voice thick with unshed tears and gratitude. He felt unbelievably weary.

The guards nodded, their movements gentle as they carried Deirdre from the gondola.

Through the cobblestone streets of Arrantown they progressed, a silent procession beneath the watchful gaze of the city's residents, hanging from windows and garrets as their eyes tracked the queen's berth wending towards the castle bridge.

The castle's looming towers cast long shadows over the procession as the sun reached its zenith. Guards in their somber livery bore Queen Deirdre with unwavering steps, her pallor stark against the rich velvet of their uniforms.

Owen trailed behind, a screw of trepidation turning in his chest with each step that brought them closer to the castle's infirmary and a prognosis for his mother's condition. Ronat walked by his side, every so often reaching out to brush her fingers against Lyr's arching back for comfort.

The doctor—a wiry man with spectacles perpetually perched on the bridge of his nose—was already awaiting them, his medical bag open and the room prepared. Owen could barely breathe as the queen was laid upon the bed, her breathing shallow, her face devoid of its usual warmth.

"Stand back, please, Your Highness," the doctor instructed, as he began his examination. Tinctures were uncorked, and the queen's temperature and blood pressure were measured as murmurs filled the room, punctuated by the clink of glass and metal.

"My mother ... Her Majesty ..." Owen began, but words failed him, the question dying in his throat.

"Give me a moment, Prince Owen," the doctor said without looking up, his hands skilful as he worked.

Ronat's hand found Owen's, squeezing tight. They waited, seconds stretching into eternity, until at last the doctor straightened, removing his spectacles to clean them on his smock.

"Queen Deirdre will recover," he declared, his voice carrying the weight of a sentence passed. "It's fatigue, nothing more. She needs rest, perhaps a few weeks of it, but she'll be herself again."

Relief crashed over Owen like a wave, and he exhaled a breath he hadn't realized he'd been holding. Beside him, Ronat's shoulders slumped, her own relief palpable. They exchanged a glance—one of hope mingled with exhaustion—as Lyr wound around their legs, her telepathic purr a soothing balm to their frayed nerves.

"Thank the ... Great Forest," Owen managed to say, before collapsing to the floor.

Chapter 24

What Lies Ahead

Despite Ronat's protestations, Owen pushed the heavy wooden door open, letting the cool evening breeze kiss his cheeks. The scent of damp earth and fresh pine filled his lungs as he stepped outside, Ronat by his side. Lyr padded alongside them, her sleek body moving with ghostly grace in the twilight shadows.

"Let's not go too far," Ronat suggested, her gaze lingering on the castle spire behind them. "You heard the doctor. You're suffering from exhaustion."

Owen nodded, his eyes tracing the familiar path that wound into the nearby kingswood. His fingers brushed against the rough bark of an old oak as they passed, imagining a semblance of strength seeping from it into him.

They walked in silence for a time, each lost in their own thoughts. The past days' events had left a mark on their spirits, like ink on parchment, indelible and stark.

"Owen," Ronat said suddenly, her voice low, "what will you do? After all this?"

He looked over at his sister, her face half-hidden in the dusk. "I've been thinking about that," he admitted. "Magic calls to me, Ronat. I can't be the prince they want, obsessed with gears and calculations. Not before, and certainly not now."

"Then don't be," she said firmly. "Be the prince you are meant to be. Or don't be a prince at all!"

"Easy for you to say," he replied with a wry smile. "You found your place among the Narra Fae. You have your magic."

"Because I chose to understand what was different in myself," she countered. "You have that same choice, Owen. Perhaps it's time for Arran to embrace a different kind of leader."

Lyr brushed against Owen's leg before scampering off into the underbrush in search of something scurrying there. Even in distraction, her thoughts mingled with his—a quiet encouragement that bolstered his resolve.

"Maybe you're right," he murmured, watching as the first stars began to pierce the deepening night sky. "It's time for a new era—one of magic and understanding, not just iron and steam."

Ronat reached out, her hand gripping his shoulder. "Whatever happens, I'll be with you," she promised. "We'll face it together."

Together, they stood, the brother who dreamed of magic and the sister who wielded it, gazing up at the heavens, pondering the unwritten future that lay spread before them like the darkened woods at their feet.

Owen and Ronat's conversation waned as the gravel crunched beneath their feet, the sound abruptly accompanied by another set of synchronized steps. They rounded a bend in the castle gardens to find Fiona and Cathal, fingers entwined, gazing into one another's eyes. The moment her eyes met those of Owen and Ronat, Fiona's cheeks flushed a deep crimson, and she swiftly unlatched her hand from Cathal's.

"Ah, don't be shy on our account," Owen teased. "The heart's yearnings are no secret within the walls of this castle."

Ronat chuckled alongside him. "Indeed, we've seen the way you steal glances at each other like magpies at a silver bauble."

Cathal, his color rising to match Fiona's, managed a sheepish grin, while Fiona composed herself with the grace of a warrior reclaiming lost ground. "Very well, then," she said. "Secrets have never been my weapon of choice."

As laughter softened the tension, Lyr, ever curious, slunk over to Fiona's side. The ser-pine's nose twitched as she nudged against the leather satchel hanging from the woman's shoulder. With a puzzled frown, Owen followed the creature's interest.

"Speaking of secrets, how are our avian companions?" he inquired, nodding toward the satchel that seemed to have slipped Fiona's mind.

"By the Cogs," Fiona gasped, the realization dawning upon her. Her hands dove into the bag, and with a gentle motion, she coaxed forth Athos and Abria. Two brown sparrows took flight, silhouetted briefly against the rising moon before vanishing into the night's embrace.

"Freedom suits them well," Ronat observed, somewhere between sincerity and irony, as her eyes followed their ascent.

Owen's eyes lingered on the fading dots in the sky, his heart a mix of hope and unease. He turned to Ronat. "What will become of them?"

Ronat shrugged. "The magic could fade, or it might endure. Nochtan's spells are capricious, his power vast. But time will reveal their fate."

Lyr's thoughts whispered into Owen's mind, a gentle nudge against his consciousness. *Pity. They would have made a fine chase as sparrows.*

"Perhaps for you," Owen replied, a smirk playing on his lips despite the gravity of their conversation. "Still, should the spell break, let's hope they're not midflight."

Laughter bubbled from Ronat, and even Fiona cracked a half-smile. They shared a brief, morbid amusement at the thought, the comfort of dark humor knitting them closer.

Behind them, the castle loomed. They moved toward it, five shadows drawn by an invisible thread of duty and destiny. Owen's steps were measured, his mind a whirlpool of memories—a stroll down a waterfall, the clash of swords, and the wondrous effects of earthspells.

Beside him, Ronat's gait held the grace of the wilds, each step as silent as the falling leaves in her Fae-touched home. Her gaze swept the path ahead, as if she could see through the earth, communing with the spirits beneath.

Behind, Fiona's sword clinked softly in its sheath. Her hand found Cathal's, their fingers intertwining like the vines that had stayed Abria—a quiet rebellion against the rigidity of caste that Arran had long upheld. His eyes met hers, not the stony gaze of a guard, but warm, full of stories yet untold.

Lyr brought up the rear, their silent chaperone, sinuous and serene, her telepathic murmurings painting pictures only Owen could see—lush meadows, moonlit hunts, the thrill of the chase. The serpine glanced at Owen, emerald eyes reflecting shared secrets and unspoken bonds. What would their next chapter together look like?

The air was thick with the weight of what they'd faced together: the lies unraveled, the loyalty forged in the crucible of chaos. Arran's future, once so sure, now seemed obscure. Whatever would be rested on their shoulders, lighter for the strength they found in one another.

Epilogue
Beneath the Oak

Beneath the sprawling branches of an ancient oak, Queen Deirdre stood in defiance of her doctors and past afflictions. Sunlight, filtered through tender green leaves, danced upon her face, revealing not hardship, but radiant health and newfound vigor. Her eyes, clear and bright as the sky above, mirrored the life that surged within her––a wellspring of vitality that had been so cruelly sapped by the machinations of those who once sought to claim her throne.

It was here, in the halls of nature's cathedral, that Fiona and Cathal would bind their lives together. The air hummed with the magic of spring—buds unfurling, flowers blooming, and all around them, the world awakening. Nature itself seemed to celebrate their union, with birdsong weaving through the rustling leaves like joyful ribbons.

Fiona, towering above her groom, strode with a warrior's grace toward the clearing that served as their altar. Her armor had been forsaken for this day, replaced by flowing fabrics that caught the breeze and sunlight in equal measure. Beside her, Cathal moved with a quiet confidence. They made a striking pair––she, the embodiment of might and fairness; he, of skill and kindness.

The two stood before one another, hands clasped as they were bound together in the ancient way, by lengths of jute cord. Their smiles told of adventures yet to come. It was a simple ceremony, devoid of pomp, yet rich in sincerity. Their vows were heartfelt promises that no one in attendance doubted.

As the final words were exchanged, and the bond of matrimony sealed with a kiss, the forest seemed to exhale in contentment. Owen's heart swelled with happiness for his guide and friend.

And there, beneath the boughs of an oak that witnessed the turning of ages, two souls joined as one, while another, young and brimming with arcane curiosity, looked on with dreams of a future where magic might flourish alongside love.

Owen twirled through the throngs of revelers with a lightness in his step that matched the spring air. Laughter bubbled from every corner of the clearing, where tables groaned under the weight of lavish dishes and sweetmeats. The scent of roasting root vegetables mingled with the floral garlands adorning the space, creating an aroma as enchanting as the fae guests themselves. Owen's eyes sparkled with delight as he observed guests from both Arran and Narra, noble and commoner alike, united in celebration.

A lively tune struck up, and dancers spilled onto the grass, their movements and dress bright spots of color against the verdant backdrop. Fiona and Cathal, now bound in marriage, led the dance, weaving between the guests. Owen watched them, his heart warming at their joy.

Later, in the quieter margins of the festivities, a small crowd gathered around Owen. They had heard whispers of his newfound proficiency, how he had studied under Ronat's tutelage and learned from a magician whose wisdom spanned the neighboring kingdom's borders. With a modest smile, Owen raised his hand, and a shower of sparks erupted from his fingertips, swirling upwards before dissipating like fireflies into the dusk. Murmurs of awe rippled through the onlookers.

"Show us more, Prince of Arran!" a young voice called out, emboldened by the spectacle.

Owen, eager to share the fruits of his study, concentrated. A moment later, the air before him shimmered, and a delicate ice sculpture materialized, capturing the last rays of the setting sun within its crystal surfaces. It was a gift of beauty, transient and ethereal.

The crowd applauded, impressed by the precision and control that belied Owen's tender years.

As the sculpture melted away, leaving only a puddle to reflect the afternoon sky, the games began. Challenges of skill and chance drew cheers, and Owen found himself swept up in a contest of riddles.

Meanwhile, Ronat weaved through the crowd, her green cloak a whisper against the grass. She had become an ambassador of sorts, a bridge between two worlds: the deep woods where magic thrived and the bustling streets of Arrantown. Her time divided, yet her purpose singular—fostering a union of nature's wild enchantments with the realm of man.

"Ronat!" Owen called out as he spotted her lingering at the periphery of the festivities. His sister turned, her smile shining amidst the revelry. "Will you return to the valley soon?"

"Tomorrow," she replied, the smile becoming tinged with sadness. "The valley calls. But ... so does Arrantown."

Owen nodded, understanding his sister's dual allegiance.

The merriment paused as Queen Deirdre's voice rose above the din, regal and clear. All eyes turned to where the queen stood, resplendent in her gown of twilight hues, the fabric shimmering like stars caught in woven silk.

"Friends, esteemed guests from near and far," Deirdre began, her gaze sweeping across the assembly. "This day marks not just the union of two kindred souls, but also the dawn of a new venture for our land."

Fiona and Cathal stepped forward, hand in hand, their faces open and ready. Deirdre smiled warmly at them.

"Under my authority, and with counsel from our noble cousins Nochtan and Boann," she continued, gesturing to the Fae royalty who bowed their heads graciously, "I hereby entrust Fiona and Cathal to lead our kingdom's commitment to harnessing sustainable energies, that we may tread lightly upon this realm which sustains us all."

Murmurs of approval rippled through the crowd.

"Thank you, Your Majesty," Fiona's voice rang strong and sure. "We vow to honor this responsibility."

"May our efforts bear fruit for generations," added Cathal, his determination matching that of his bride.

As the applause died down, Owen looked on, his spirit alight. Magic and technology, once seen as opposing forces, were finding harmony under his family's guidance. And within him, the seeds of change promised to flourish in ways none could yet foresee.

Late in the evening, Owen watched the Arran children playing with their Fae counterparts. True magic hung in the air, palpable. The young ones lifted pebbles with mere flicks of their fingers, turning them into fluttering butterflies that danced away on the breeze. A boy, no older than seven, whispered to a wilting flower, its petals reinvigorating to a vibrant pink before everyone's eyes.

A pair of sparrows above argued, oblivious to the wonder below. Their banter was a sharp contrast to the harmony of the gathering. Owen hardly noticed them, nor the squabble they were acting out.

"Beautiful, isn't it?" a voice said beside him, soft yet clear.

Owen turned. She was the one who was beautiful—her eyes a kaleidoscope of greens and blues, hair cascading like a waterfall of night. Lysandra, her name echoed in his mind before she even introduced herself.

"Magic always is."

"Can you do this?" she asked, extending her hand. A sprig of lavender bloomed from her palm, unfurling as if coaxed by the sun itself.

"Something like it," Owen admitted, focusing inward to draw forth his power. A small orb of light formed over his outstretched hand, casting prismatic colors onto Lysandra's fascinated face.

"An orb of illumination," she mused. "You have a gentle touch with magic."

"'A gentle touch'? Is that a kind way of saying that I'm still a beginner?"

Lysandra laughed as Owen grinned.

"Ronat taught me," he said with a shrug, watching the orb dissipate into a shower of harmless sparks. "I much prefer it to machines and gears."

"Ah, the sister who walks between worlds," Lysandra nodded, understanding. "To be born of one realm and embrace another, it's a rare gift."

"Like yours?"

"Perhaps," she smiled, a secret lighting her features. "We Fae are born of magic, but to master it, we must learn, just as you do."

"Will you show me?" The question escaped him, bold and hopeful.

"Only if you'll share your learning, Prince of Arran." Her tone was teasing, yet sincere.

"Deal," he agreed without hesitation, excitement bubbling within him.

"Then let us begin." And with that, Lysandra reached out, taking his hand.

The sparrows flew off, their quarrel interrupted but not forgotten.

THE END

Printed in Great Britain
by Amazon